SV

Bulgarian Folk Tales

Selected, arranged, and rendered in English by

Ivona Hecht

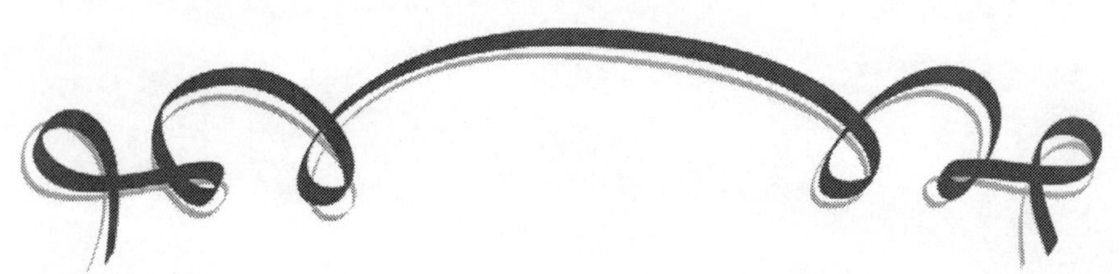

SWEET DREAMS

Bulgarian Folk Tales

ISBN 954-28-0108-4
EAN-13 978-954-28-0108-5

CONTENTS

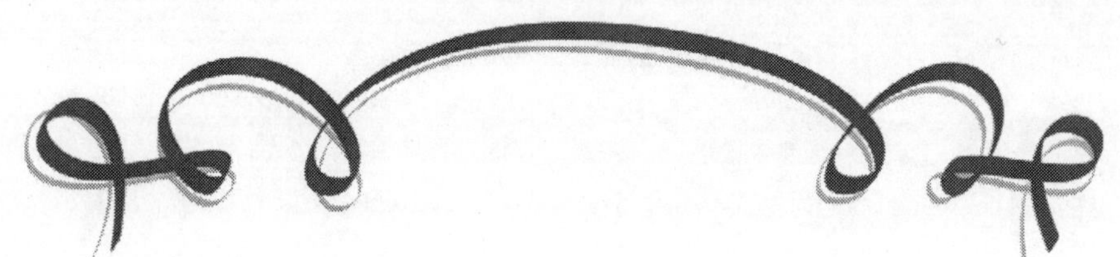

TALES ABOUT MAGIC

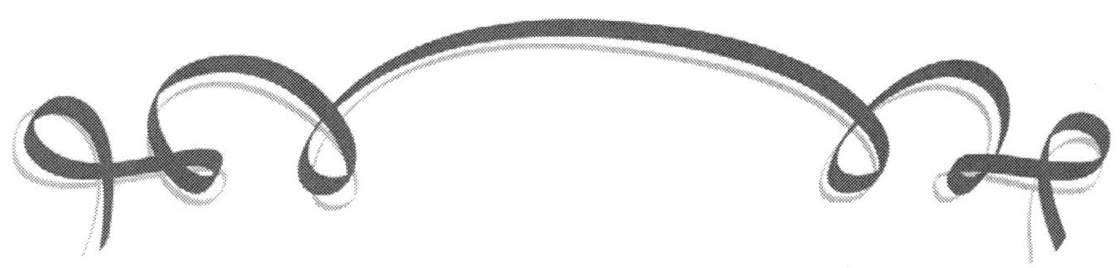

LIVE WATER

Once upon a time, there lived a king. He had three sons: the eldest was married, the middle one was engaged, and the youngest was single. One day, a mysterious illness befell the king. Many doctors and healers examined him and finally gave their verdict, "You'll get better only if you drink live water. There's no other cure!"

The king gathered his sons and asked them to go in search of live water. They loved their father deeply and immediately set forth on the long journey. After a long day's ride, they reached a mountain where the road split in three and a three-spout fountain stood in the middle. The sign above the fountain read that whoever took the left fork would come back unscathed; whoever took the right fork, might not be so lucky, but whoever took the middle one, would face certain death. The youngest brother read the sign to his siblings and proposed, "We'll split here. You, the eldest among us, will take the left road. You have a home and a family, and they need you. You, my middle brother, are engaged. Take the right fork, and you'll have a chance to come back alive to your fiancée. I'm

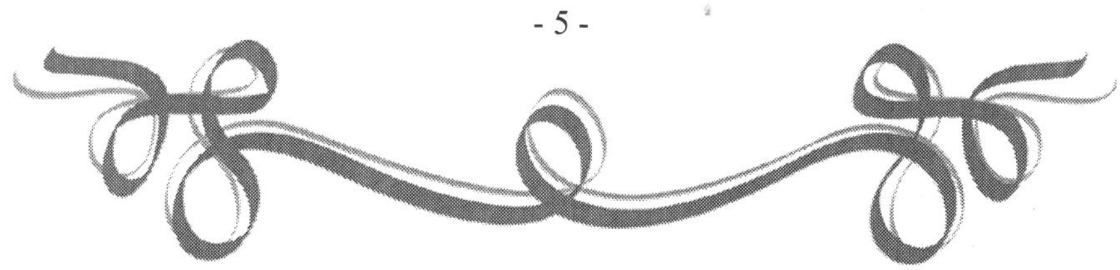

single and have nobody at home, so it's fitting that I take the middle road."

Before taking their leave, each brother left a ring under the fountain's foundation. They agreed that whoever came back alive, would take his ring back so the others would know live water had been found.

The youngest brother traveled along the middle road until it came to a wild, rocky desert. He meandered among the boulders the whole day and by nightfall was completely parched. In his search of water, he found a ravine where something sparkled down below. "Great, a creek!" rejoiced the boy, and quickly went to investigate. What he saw wasn't a creek but a huge snake covered with silvery scales.

"I'll kill the snake and drink its blood, that should quench my thirst," he thought, grabbed his bow and arrow and aimed at the snake. As soon as the sharp point hit the snake, dark blood came gushing out, and the serpent said in a man's voice, "May you be blessed, young man, for relieving me from the pain! This dark blood had been poisoning me for ages! Now I'm cured! From this day on, you'll be my brother. How can I repay you?"

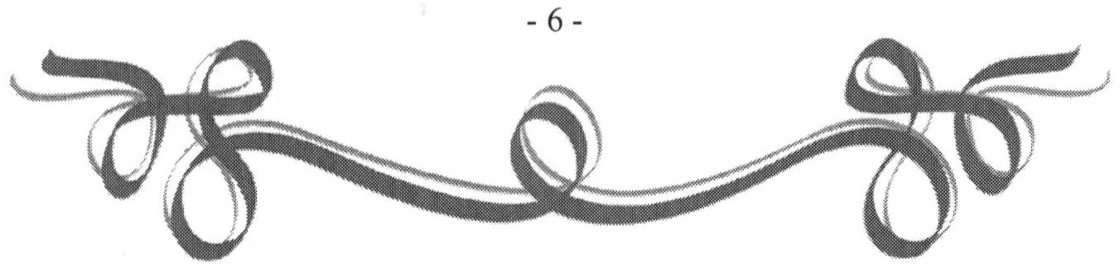

“I want nothing for myself,“ replied the boy, “but do you know where I can find live water for my ailing father?”

“You ask a big favor, brother,“ said the snake. “Come to my house and be my servant for three days, then I’ll tell you.”

The boy agreed. On the morning of the third day, the snake handed him one of its skin scales and said, “Take this scale and go toward the sunset. In three days, you’ll reach a dried-up well where my brother lives. He’s half-man, half-snake. Ask him, and he’ll direct you to the live water.”

It took the boy three long days to reach the dried-up well. The half-man and half-snake creature came out and shouted angrily, “Who are you and what are you doing here where no human has dared since I was born?”

The boy handed him the scale and the creature was so happy that he wanted to reward him.

“I don’t want anything for myself,” the boy said, “but tell me, do you know where I can find live water for my ailing father? If I don’t take it to him, he’ll die.”

“You want a big reward, my dear!” exclaimed the half-man/half-snake. ”Stay here and be my servant for two days, then I’ll tell you.” When the two days were up, he took the boy to the road

and pointed to a big mountain in the distance, “On top of that mountain is the palace of the Fire Dragon. You’ll find live water there.”

The boy was eager to leave immediately but the half-man/half-snake stopped him, “Do you know why I kept you here for two days?” The boy said he didn’t. “The Fire Dragon and his people sleep only two days in the year; you had to wait for these two days to come. Now follow this road and it’ll take you there in half a day. Everyone in the palace will be deeply asleep. Don’t let their open eyes scare you as they always sleep like that. When you get past them, climb to the highest tower and look for the jugs of live water on the floor. Grab one and run before the guards wake up.”

The boy did as he was told and reached the palace. He was about to grab only one jug of live water and leave but decided to get three just in case. He was curious how the Fire Dragon lived and on his way out peeked into an open bedroom. There, on a gilded bed, slept a beautiful girl, the Fire Dragon’s daughter. The boy reached down, took the ring off her finger, and left quietly.

When he got to the fountain, he saw that all the rings were still there and wondered what had happened to his brothers. He hid one of the live-water jugs by the fountain, picked the other two, and

set forth to look for his brothers. After a whole night's ride, the boy reached a remote kingdom where the eldest brother was being kept prisoner in a dark dungeon. The boy begged the king to free his brother, and he agreed to do so if the boy could cure his ailing daughter. He sprinkled the princess with live water, she immediately got better, and the king set the eldest brother free.

The two brothers continued their travel and sometime later found their third brother. He had been wounded in a battle and was dying. They sprinkled him with live water and saved his life. Afterwards, the three brothers went back to the fountain together, collected their rings, and started toward home.

"How are we going to cure our father, we used up all the live water," the elder brothers wondered.

"Don't worry," said the youngest, "we have another jug left. I hid it just in case."

At some point during their journey, the brothers got thirsty. They saw an old well on the side of the road and decided that one of them should go down and get some water. The eldest brother offered to go but the youngest objected and climbed down instead.

"Let's leave him down there!" the two brothers decided. "If he comes home with us, our father will love him more than he loves

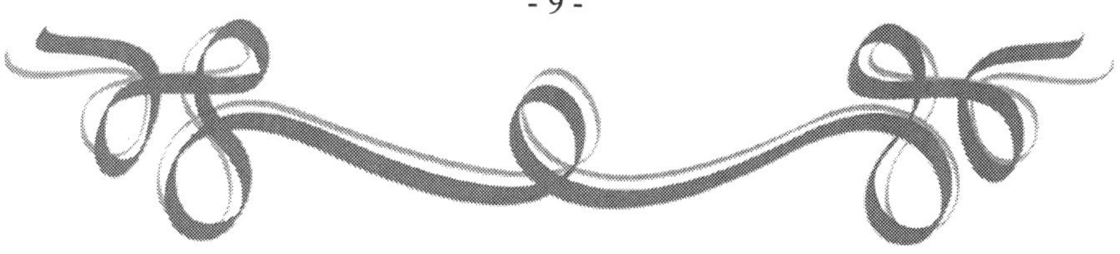

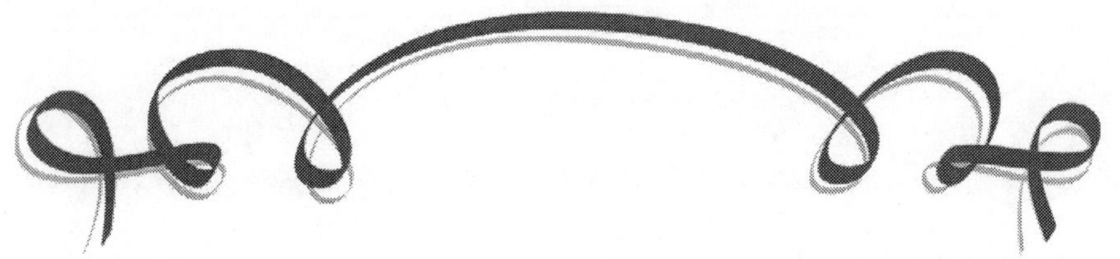

us because he found the live water, and our father may disinherit us."

The elder brothers hurried back to the palace, gave their father the live water, and he was instantly cured. He asked about his youngest son, and the two brothers said that they had split at the fountain and had no idea where he had gone.

At this same moment, a traveling merchant stopped by the old well to water his horses. As he pulled the bucket, it felt very heavy. To his surprise, the man saw a boy holding on to it. "What are you, a man or a ghost?" he asked.

"A man," replied the boy.

"How did you find yourself down there?"

"I don't remember who I am!" cried the boy. "I bent over to get some water, fell in, and couldn't climb out. Since then, I remember nothing."

After giving it some thought, the merchant offered, "Would you like to be my son? I have no children to help me in my work. You'll be my partner." The boy agreed, and they started traveling together.

While all this was going on, the guards in the Fire Dragon's palace woke up. His daughter, too, woke up and realized something

of hers was missing but couldn't tell exactly what. Nobody thought about counting the jugs of live water up on the terrace. The princess went to her father and said, "Father, let's prepare lavish gifts and take them to our neighboring kingdoms. I know how we'll find out what was stolen." The Fire Dragon followed her advice and prepared many amazing presents, the most exquisite of which was a tiny church no bigger than a human palm. Loaded with all the gifts, the princess started visiting the neighboring kingdoms and told everyone, "I don't want presents in return. All I want is to know if anyone in your kingdom knows the Fire Dragon's palace. Has anyone been there?"

Nobody knew. The same thing happened in the palace where the three brothers' father was the king. Nobody had ever heard of such a place.

Suddenly, the king remembered the traveling merchant who went all over the land, and sent his emissaries to bring him. "You've been to all places and kingdoms, to all towns and villages," he told the merchant. "You must know the Fire Dragon's palace. I give you three days to think about it."

The merchant went home all shaky and pale. As the day wore on, his condition got worse and worse.

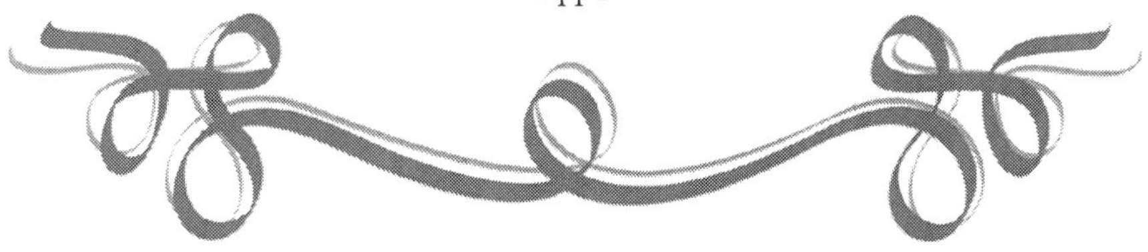

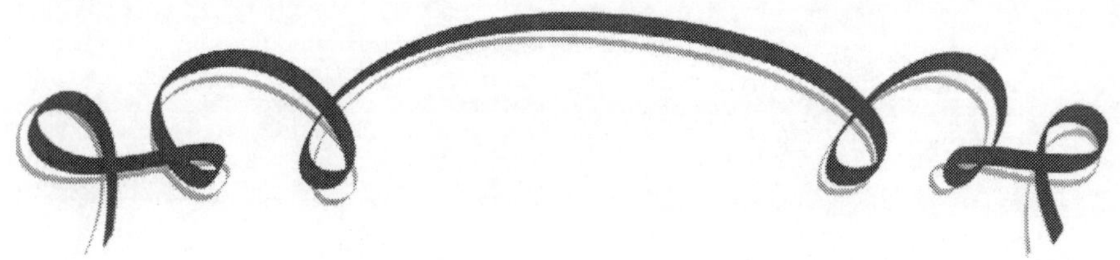

"Are you upset because you took me in and gave me a home?" inquired the boy. "If so, please tell me, and I'll leave right away."

"No, my dear, you're my only true joy," replied the merchant. "There's something else. The king gave me three days to find out where the Fire Dragon's palace was. If I can't, he'll have me killed."

"Don't worry," said the boy cheerfully, "Tell the king to gather his family. I'll go over and tell them where the Fire Dragon lives."

"God bless you, my son!" cried the merchant. "I knew I saved your life for a good reason!" And immediately he sent a letter to the king informing him that he had found someone who knew where the Fire Dragon's palace was, but that he wanted to give his answer before the whole royal family. The next morning, the boy put on the ring he had stolen from the Fire Dragon's daughter and went to the palace where everyone was waiting. He sat across from them, put his ringed hand in full view, and started telling them his story from the beginning. He told them how there was a king who had three sons, how he fell ill and sent them to find live water, and how the older ones tricked their younger brother and left him to die.

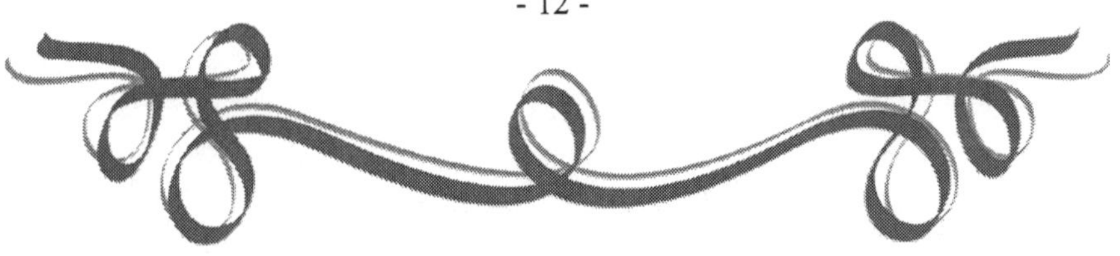

The Fire Dragon's daughter recognized her ring on the boy's finger and, to everyone's surprise, shouted that she knew him.

"And then the merchant pulled the boy out of the old well and took him in like a true son," the boy continued. "That boy knew where the Fire Dragon lived."

"Do you know the palace?" asked the king, beginning to understand what was going on.

"Yes, he does, Your Highness!" cried the Fire Dragon's daughter. "He's wearing my ring! I'm the Fire Dragon's daughter, and from this day on, I'll be your daughter-in-law!" She told the king and queen how someone had sneaked into the palace while everyone was asleep and had stolen three jugs of live water and her ring.

The very next day, the king gave his youngest son a lavish wedding where he married the Fire Dragon's daughter, and everyone lived happily ever after.

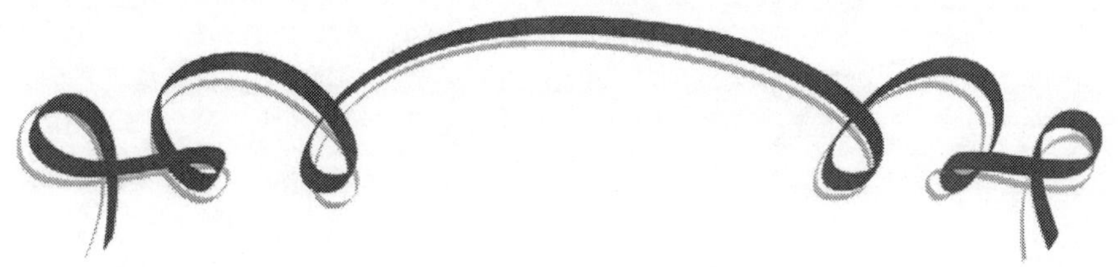

THE POWER OF SISTERLY LOVE

Once upon a time, there lived an old man who had forty sons and one blind daughter. Every morning, the blind girl made all the beds and cooked huge meals for the whole family. The father had a big wheatfield, which bore grains as big as cranberries, and worked there night and day to put food on the table. An apple tree stood in the middle of the field, and a little brook ran beside it. Fall came, the leaves turned, and the tree bore fruit. The old man gathered the grain for seed and led his forty plows of oxen out to the field. The work was long and tiring, and when it was done, the old man went home and fell ill from exhaustion. His daughter made him a special potion from bitter roots but it didn't help. When he felt his end was near, the father called for his sons, "My dear children, I'm going to a faraway place from which nobody has ever come back. Come near so I can give you a kiss."

When they had all said good-bye, the father continued, "Remember that our wheatfield gives the best grains. Work it together, live in peace, and don't quarrel. Who'll go now to bring

me a jug of cool water from the brook? I want to drink some before I die. “

The sons set out together with forty clay jugs, but when they got to the brook, instead of getting water, they began measuring the wheatfield.

“Why are you measuring the wheatfield?” asked the youngest brother.

“So we can divide it among us,” they said. The brothers started dividing the wheatfield and got into a big fight. There was a lot of shouting and hitting, and all the clay jugs got broken.

“What are my sons doing?” wondered the old man.

“Fighting over the wheatfield, Father,” replied the blind girl.

“Did they bring any water for me?”

“No, Father.”

The father sighed sadly and pronounced, “May they all turn into moles who dig the earth since they’re so greedy for it!”

The father’s curse reached the sons and they were turned immediately into moles who scampered all over the field, dug holes, and disappeared underground.

Shortly after that, the father passed away. After the funeral, the blind sister went to the wheatfield looking for her brothers. She

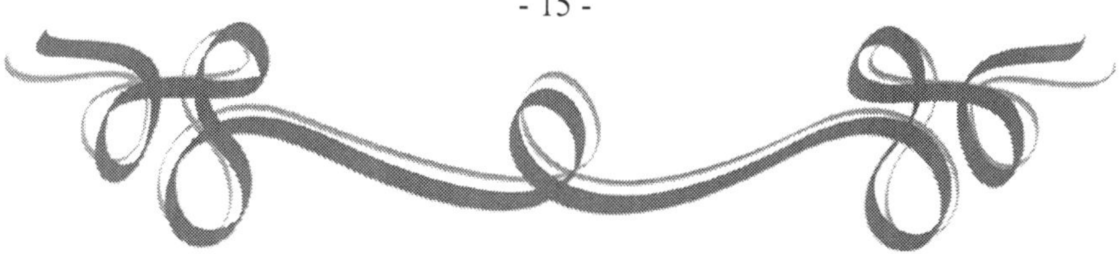

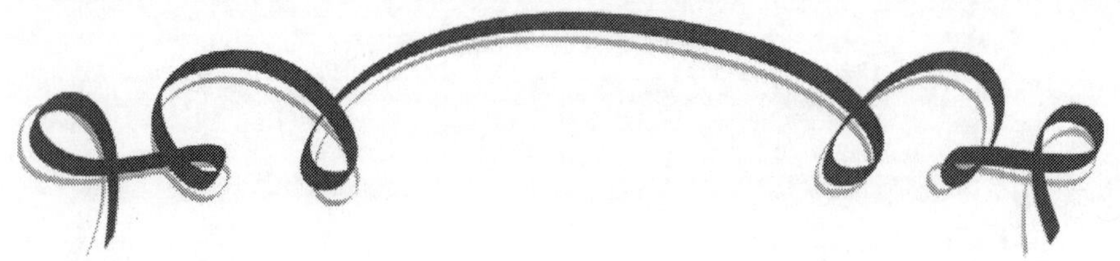

called out their names but nobody answered. Feeling sad, she sat under the apple tree and started crying. Suddenly, a little lizard came out of the brook and told her, “Don’t cry, your brothers are alive.”

“Where are they?” she asked. “Why aren’t they answering me?”

“They’re in the Lower Land.”

“How do you know that?”

“The water told me. It comes from great depths and knows everything.”

“How do I get there?” wondered the girl.

“I’ll tell you how. At the lower end of the field, there’s a dried-up well. Jump in the bucket and go to the bottom. There, you’ll see a huge boulder. Lift it, and underneath you’ll see a big stone stairwell leading to the Lower Land. Follow it all the way.”

The girl gathered all the apples from the tree in a big basket. There were exactly 40 of them, one for each of her brothers. She found the dried-up well, jumped in the bucket, and went all the way to the bottom, reached the stone stairwell, and started climbing down. For twenty weeks, she never stopped. She was starving but didn’t reach for the apples because they were meant for her brothers.

On the first day of the twenty-first week, the girl reached the Lower Land.

“Who are you looking for?” asked an elderly woman.

“My forty brothers. Do you know where they are?”

“They’re here. I’m to keep them locked in a small house. Three times a day, I feed them salty soil, and when they get really thirsty, I give them cups of water. They hold them in their front paws but as soon as the cups get near their lips, the bottoms fall out and the water spills. Your brothers can never quench their thirst. They must be getting punished for a great sin, but I don’t know what it is.”

“Please take me to them,” pleaded the blind girl. When she entered the house, the moles began whimpering pitifully.

“Would you allow me to give them an apple each?” she asked.

“Ycs,” rcplicd thc old woman.

The girl gave each mole a ripe apple. They hungrily bit into the fruits and instantly turned back into people. Being blind, she couldn’t see them, but heard their voices and wept from joy. The youngest brother ate only half of his apple and offered her the other. As soon as she took a bite, her eyesight returned. Her brothers were

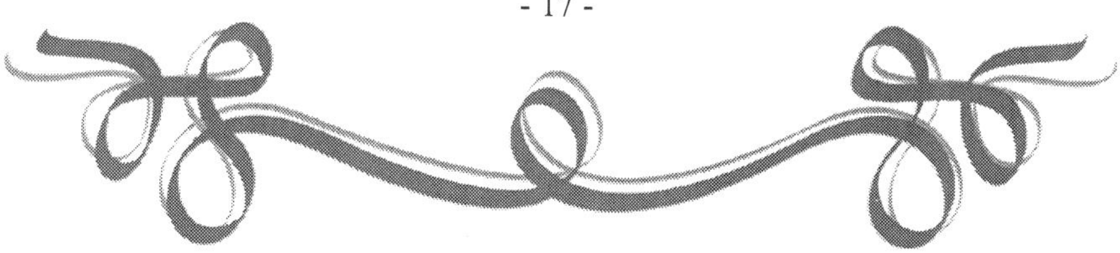

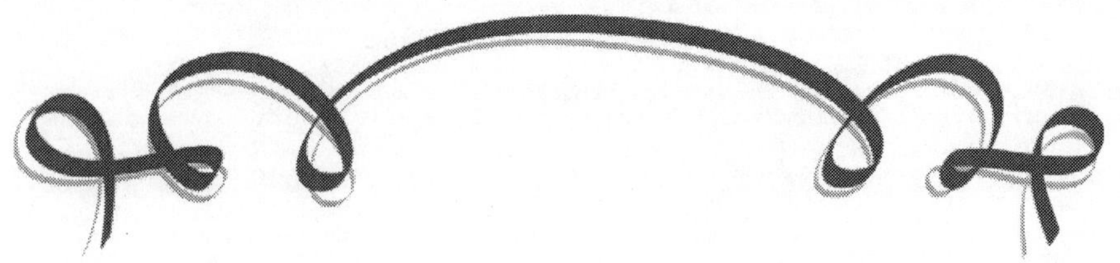

overcome with happiness not to be moles anymore, and their sister couldn't get enough of looking at them for the first time.

Slowly, they started the long climb up the stairwell. On the first day of the twenty-first week, they reached the top of the old well and got out. Before their eyes, their father's wheatfield looked golden under the cover of the ripened grains. The brothers grabbed their sickles and reaped the abundant harvest. Their sister baked a whole oven full of bread and gave the loaves to the poor in memory of her late father. A second batch of bread was eaten by her brothers who, from that day on, lived together in peace and harmony, as brothers always should.

THE MAGIC RING

Once upon a time, in a small village surrounded by dense woods, there lived a poor woman with her son. He wanted to help bring food to the table and so started hunting with a bow and arrow. Before long, he had become famous as an experienced archer.

In a neighboring town, there was a man who needed just such an accurate marksman, so he went to the boy's village and organized a shooting contest, whose winner would become a wealthy man. For a target, the man arranged three eggs and challenged the archers to pierce them with a single arrow. The boy was the only one who managed to do that, and the man was very impressed. He offered him a job as his personal marksman, and the two of them left the village soon after that.

They walked for a long time and finally reached a high mountain, at the side of which gaped a huge, dark cave.

"This cave is the dwelling of a scary dragon, and nobody dares come near," the man explained. "The dragon comes out only once a year to drink water. See this river? The dragon sucks all the water out, and it stays dry for nine months. While drinking, the

dragon dips all of his nine heads in at once, but then pulls them out one by one. That's when you'll shoot him. If you can do that, I'll make you very rich."

"That's easy," agreed the boy.

"Great! Let me tie you to this tree so the windstorm doesn't blow you away. The dragon always raises a storm when he breathes."

In a little while, the dragon appeared, cloaked in thunder and fire, and started drinking from the river. When he was done and started pulling his heads out, the boy skillfully shot through each and every one of them. When the dragon fell, the water came gushing out and filled the river again.

"Now go inside the cave," instructed the man. "You'll see a big rusty ring hanging on the wall. Bring it to me, but be very careful! You'll hear beautiful voices and heavenly music. Don't pay any attention to them. Grab the ring and run."

The boy did as he was told and was almost all the way back to the opening when a particularly beautiful melody made him slow his pace. Suddenly, a huge boulder fell and barred the way out, trapping him inside the cave. A couple of days later, the boy got hungry and decided to dig the ground for something to chew. The

earth was rocky, so he punched it with the ring. Immediately, a giant materialized from thin air.

"I'm at your services, Master!" he said.

"I'm very hungry. Bring me some food and water!" ordered the boy.

"Right away! Go to sleep now. When you wake up, food and water will be waiting for you."

Indeed, when the boy woke up shortly, he saw many plates full of tasty foods and a jug of chilled water, but the giant was gone. A few days went by. The boy finished all the food and water and soon got hungry and thirsty again. He touched the ring to the ground, and the giant appeared again. The boy ordered more food and water and a comfortable bed to sleep on. When he awoke, he was in the dragon's palace, covered by piles of golden coins. At that point, the boy had figured out that he could summon the giant at any time by simply touching the ring to the ground, and started calling him with all kinds of requests. After some time had passed, the boy started missing his mother and called the genie again.

"What can I do for you, Master?"

"Take me and all this gold to my house. My mother must be worried sick about me."

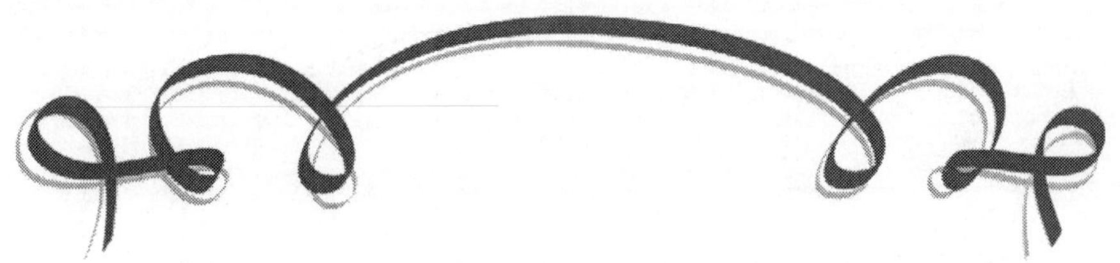

After the boy fell asleep, the genie fulfilled his request, and soon, mother and son were reunited. Thanks to all the gold coins, their life became very pleasant.

Months and months went by. One day, the boy, now a grown young man, decided to look for a bride. He asked his mother to go to the palace and ask for the princess's hand in marriage.

"How could I do that?" she wondered. "I used to beg in front of the palace while you were gone."

"You were poor then, but now, you're richer than the king himself," assured her the boy.

When the woman got to the palace, the guards spotted her and told the king, who immediately sent her some money and food.

"God has provided me with food and riches. I'm not here to beg but to see our king," she explained.

When the king heard this, he had the guards bring her before him, and she explained her mission.

"That's all very good," the king said, "but you're poor, and my daughter's accustomed to an affluent lifestyle."

"We're not poor, Your Highness! We might even be richer than you. I was begging before not because I needed money but because I wanted to meet with you."

"If you're telling the truth, I'll give your son my daughter's hand in marriage. Tell him that he must first build a palace for them to live in. It must be more beautiful than mine. He has three days to do that."

When she got home, her son asked what had happened, and she explained.

"There's no way we can build a gorgeous palace in just three days!"

"Don't worry, Mother, I'll find a way!" reassured her the boy. He went outside, touched the ring to the ground, and summoned the giant.

"I'm at your service, Master! What can I do for you?"

"Build me a palace, bigger and more beautiful than the king's. You have three days."

When the boy woke up the next morning, their house had disappeared, and a gorgeous palace stood in its place. His mother sent the news to the king who promptly replied, "Now tell your son to build a road from his palace to mine. Tell him to make it so smooth that an egg could roll all the way without breaking."

When the boy heard the new request, he summoned the giant again. On the third day, the road was ready, stretching smooth and

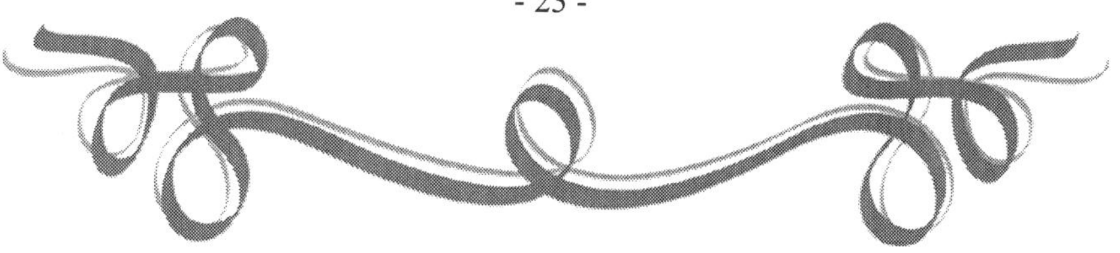

shiny between the two palaces. When an egg was rolled on it, it went smoothly all the way.

The king was stumped what else to ask for, so he sent for the boy's mother and told her that her son was to build a special garden. There had to be all kinds of trees known to man: trees in blossom, trees whose fruit was just ripening, other trees which bore fruit, and still others from which the fruit had already been picked.

"You can't possibly create a garden like that!" she said to her son. "Only God can do that."

The boy told her not to worry and summoned the giant. As always, the giant told him to doze off. Upon waking, the boy saw the most beautiful garden full of unusual trees. Some of them were blooming and their fragrance wafted in the air; some were heavily laden with fruit; some were just starting to ripen, and still others were barren as if it was winter. When the king saw the garden, he admitted defeat and agreed to the marriage between the boy and his daughter.

From that day on, the boy, now a handsome young man, became a royal advisor. He went to the palace every day and left his ring at home. Nobody but him knew the power of the ancient rusty piece.

Meanwhile, the man, who had once upon a time hired the young man for his personal archer, found out about his wealth and got very jealous. Knowing that the young man's wealth was all due to the old ring, he made plans to buy it and started going around town pretending to search for antique jewelry. When he asked at the palace, the young man's wife remembered the old rusty ring hanging on the wall. Since she considered it an eyesore, getting some money for it seemed like an excellent idea. The man was very happy to get the coveted ring. He hid it under his tongue and hurried away. When he got to a secluded spot, the man pulled out the ring and summoned the giant.

"What do you wish me to do, Master?" he asked.

"Take this palace to the end of the earth where neither man, nor beast has set foot before."

The giant told him that he would carry out the order as soon as the man dozed off. Meanwhile, the young man returned from the king's palace and was astonished to find an empty space where his home used to be. He went back to the king and told him that he had lost everything and the princess was gone. The king got angry and ordered him to find his daughter and bring her back, or else he would lose his life. The young man had no choice but to set off on a

search around the world, looking high and low for his wife and home. Sometime during the journey, he saw a stray kitten and took it along for company. One day, the kitten started chasing a rat. The rat looked at the young man and pleaded in a human voice, "Save me, and I'll do you a favor! Save me, and I'll bring you good luck!" The young man was surprised but held the kitten back and saved the rat's life.

"What can I do for you to repay you?" the rat asked.

"Tell me if you know where my wife and my palace are?"

"I don't, but since I'm the king of all mice, I'll gather them and ask. Someone is bound to know something."

When all mice got together, the rat asked if anyone had seen the princess and the palace. Nobody had, but they soon discovered that one of the field mice still hadn't shown up, and the rat thought that she might have the answer. When she finally arrived, the field mouse apologized for being late. She had good news as she lived in the very palace where the princess was held. She told the rat that the new palace owner always carried the ring under his tongue and took it out only during meals when he put it on the table.

"In that case," said the rat, "it should be very easy for you to steal the ring from him. Dip your tail in honey, swirl it around in

black pepper, and tickle his nose with it after he falls asleep tonight. When he sneezes, the ring will come right out."

A couple of days later, the field mouse came back and brought the ring. The young man was overjoyed and immediately summoned the giant.

"I'm at your services, Master!" the giant said.

"Cover this field in loaves of bread!" the young man ordered.

Suddenly, the huge field was covered in loaves of freshly baked bread, and everyone in the mouse kingdom ate until they all had their fill. The young man then ordered the giant to take the palace, along with his wife and all their riches, and bring them all back to where they belonged. When they got there, the young man went to the seashore and threw the old ring in the water where it immediately sank into the deep.

The young couple soon had several adorable children and they all lived happily thereafter.

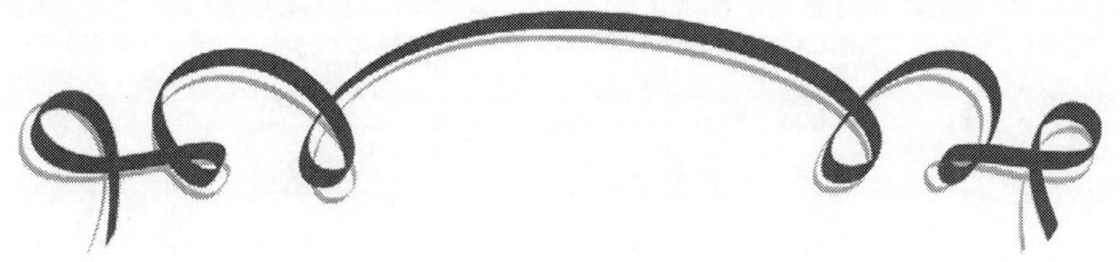

THE ELDERLY COUPLE AND THEIR LITTLE DUCKLING

Once upon a time, there lived an old married couple. They had no children and were all alone. One day, they were sitting by the fire, lamenting their lost youth.

"Oh, dear, what are we going to do from now on?" The old woman's sad voice carried in the small house. "Our eyes can't see any more, our legs can't carry us, and our hands don't obey us like they used to. How are we going to manage with nobody to help us?"

Her elderly husband silently shrugged his shoulders.

If we had a little girl, things would be different," the wife continued.

Just then, the moon was right outside their window. She heard their conversation, and her beautiful face darkened with sadness.

"You know, dear," suggested the woman. "Maybe our luck's due to change. Go put the old landing net in the river. Whatever you catch, it will be our daughter."

The old man went to the river and put the net in. After looking at it for a while, he dozed off and didn't wake up until the

next morning. When he checked the net, it was full of weeds. Nestled among them was a cute duckling with silvery feet and a golden beak. The old man took the duckling home and happily called his wife to see it.

"Oh, what a sweetie!" cried the woman and patted its wet feathers. "It can't help us in any way but it will be our companion. I'm so tired of us being alone. Say something, dear!" she urged the little bird. It looked at her and issued a soft quack.

"You're precious!" exclaimed the woman. "Nobody else makes such cute sounds." She took an old pot, settled the duckling inside, and fed it a bit of grain porridge. "This is your new home, darling!" she continued. "We're going out now to gather some mushrooms. You stay here and don't get out because there's a big, nasty weasel lurking out there. Take good care of yourself because you're our little girl now."

The elderly people put on their coats, grabbed a couple of baskets, and went out. As soon as their footsteps died down, the duckling jumped out of the pot, spread its wings, flapped them three times, and quacked four times. As soon as it did that, all its feathers came off, and a beautiful girl emerged in its place. She had golden blond hair and her feet were encased in dainty silver slippers. She looked

around the small house and set to work. She swept and mopped the floor, brought fresh water from the well, watered all the flowers in the garden, and started a pot of mushroom soup. While the soup was cooking, she took a roll of soft cotton cloth from the chest under the bed and quickly fashioned two shirts, decorating them with beautiful embroidery. By the time the shirts were ready and the soup was cooked, the day had come to an end. At sundown, the girl waved her arms three times, quacked four times, and turned back into a duckling.

When the old couple returned home, they were amazed to see the clean house, the new shirts, and the pot of delicious soup simmering on the fire. "Who had done that? Who had started the fire in the fireplace? Who had sewn those beautiful shirts?" they wondered. The duckling looked at them and kept silent. The old people were tired so they quickly ate their dinner and went to bed. The next morning, they decided to go into the woods and gather some wild berries. When they returned in the evening, the house was gleaming, a big pot of bean soup was simmering in the fireplace, and two brand new overcoats were hanging on a hanger. They were made of soft wool and trimmed in rabbit fur.

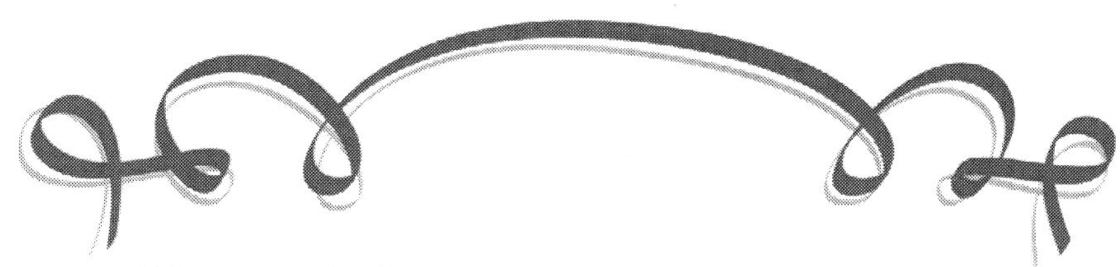

“I’ve never had a more delicious bean soup in my life!” exclaimed the old woman.

“We need to find out who comes here and does all this,“ suggested her husband. “But how can we do that?”

“We’ll pretend we’re leaving the house tomorrow morning, but we’ll hide up on the roof instead and look through the chimney.”

The next day, they did as planned and saw how the duckling turned into a girl. She immediately got busy sifting flour, kneading bread, and making new slippers for them. “Oh, we’re so lucky! We’ll be living the good life in our old age!” they rejoiced. A little later, the girl went outside to pick up a broom.

“I don’t want our daughter turning back into a duckling! I want her to stay as she is!“ said the woman.

“What can we do?”

“Let’s burn her duck outfit! Then she’ll stay a girl forever.” They quickly slid down the chimney into the kitchen, grabbed the duck wings and feathers, and threw them into the fire. Just at that moment, the girl came back inside and saw them. “What have you done?!” she cried. “You’ve burned my feathers! How am I supposed to circle the sky without wings?”

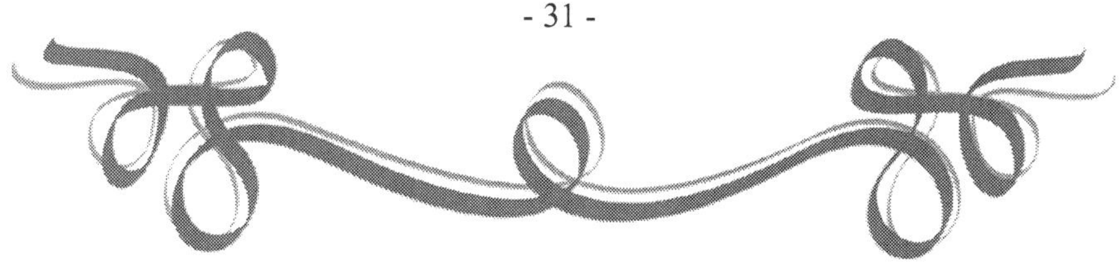

The elderly couple was astonished. “Why would you need to circle the sky?”

The girl started wringing her hands and crying. “You don’t understand! I’m not really a duckling! I’m the one who lights up the sky at night. I’m the Moon. I was peeking through your window that night, and I felt sorry for you. The old medicine woman from the forest told me that I was to shine from the sky at night, but that I could come down to help you during the day. She said that I’d need duck wings for that and gathered all the living creatures that could fly. ‘Our moon wants to help a lonely old couple during the day, and she needs wings. Please, give her a feather each! I’ll put your feathers together to make wings.’ When she gave me the wings, the medicine woman told me to guard them very carefully because I would not be able to light up the sky without them ever again.”

“Goodness!” fretted the old woman. “What are we going to do now?”

“The two of you will now go around the forest gathering feathers from each and every flying creature. When you have enough, go to the medicine woman. She lives in an old shack at the end of the woods. Ask her to make another pair of wings, and bring

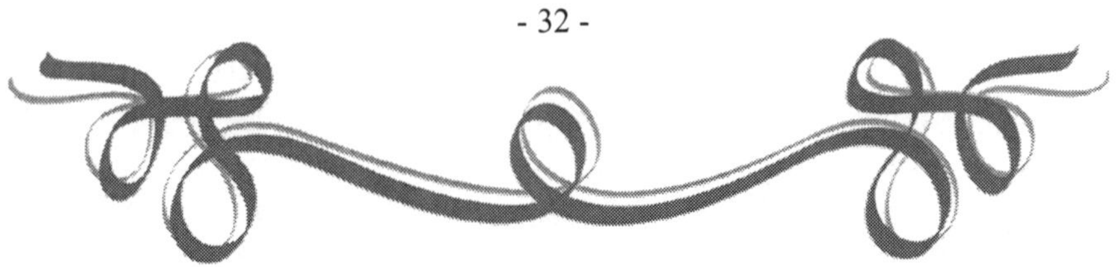

them to me. I'll be hiding in that cave over there, waiting for you." With these words, the girl jumped to her feet and left.

The couple had no choice but to go around the forest begging each little bird for a feather. They often stopped to rest and looked up at the sky, hoping to see the moon, but it was always dark and covered with clouds. After seven days, the man and the woman had collected feathers from every single bird except the blue jay. "Why should I give you one?" the bird grumbled. "My tail's the prettiest of all! What will it look like with a missing feather?"

The old couple begged and pleaded with the blue jay for three days until it reluctantly agreed to give them a tiny feather. In exchange, the vain bird demanded to be given a pearl necklace. The elderly people had no such treasures and felt very sad. Hot tears started falling from the woman's eyes. When the drops touched the ground, they didn't disappear but, instead, turned into beautiful shiny pearls. She gathered them into a necklace and put it around the blue jay's neck. The bird plucked the tiniest feather from its tail and grudgingly dropped it to where the two people were standing. The little feather got caught in the wind and started flying away faster and faster. The elderly couple chased it the whole day. They jumped over hills and got pricked by thorns but finally caught the

tiny feather and brought it to the medicine woman. She frowned at their request for a new pair of wings but eventually took all the feathers and set to work. When the duck wings were ready, the elderly people took them and headed to the cave where the girl was hiding.

"Come out, come out, dear!" they shouted. "We have your wings for you!"

The girl came out, put the wings on, and turned into a duckling that quickly flew up toward the sky. A moment later, all people around the world were looking up and admiring the beautiful silvery moon shining from above. Nobody had ever seen a more beautiful sight.

THE THREE BROTHERS AND THE GOLDEN APPLE

Once upon a time, in a charming little house with a big orchard, there lived a mother with her three sons. Right in the middle of the orchard there stood a tall apple tree, which bore only one golden apple a year. The mother and her three sons wanted very much to taste it but never could because somebody kept sneaking in during the night and eating the fruit. When the boys grew up, the eldest brother decided to guard the apple.

"Mother, give me a knife and a bag of walnuts," he asked. "I'll go watch the tree tonight." He sat under the apple tree and got so carried away cracking the walnuts that he never noticed the huge dragon sneaking past and snatching the fruit off the tree.

The next year, the middle brother decided to try his luck. Just like his elder brother before him, he cracked and ate walnuts all night long and also missed the dragon when it swooped and stole the apple.

On the third year, it was the youngest brother's turn. Unlike his two brothers, he took only a knife and nothing else, climbed up the apple tree, and sat on a big branch to wait for the dragon. When

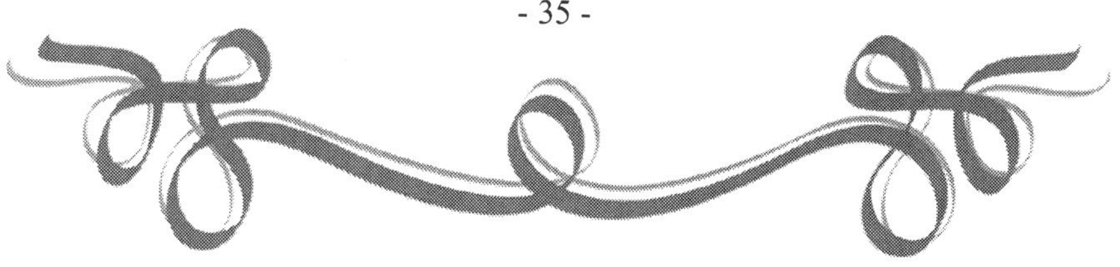

it showed up, the boy threw his knife and managed to wound the beast. It immediately flew away with a thundering roar. The boy picked the apple off the tree and took it home to his mother.

"Mother, I'm going to find the dragon and slay it," he said. "If I don't, it's going to come back next year and steal another apple."

His brothers decided to accompany him, and the three of them went in search of the beast. The trail of blood droplets led them to a deep crevice. The brothers decided to tie themselves to a rope and go down. The eldest one went first but got scared and signaled to be pulled back up. The middle brother followed but he also got frightened, tugged on the rope, and his two brothers pulled him to the surface. The youngest brother was next. He tied the rope around his waist and lowered himself all the way down. When he got there, he untied the rope and started walking around. After a while, he reached the house where the dragon lived with its three daughters. Through the window, he saw that two of the girls were playing with beautiful golden apples while the third one sat empty-handed. He knocked on the door and asked them to let him in.

"We can't let you in!" the youngest girl exclaimed. "Go away, stranger! Our mother's very angry and will eat you alive if

she finds you here! She usually brings us golden apples to play with, but this year she came back with a nasty wound and no apple."

The youngest brother was adamant, "I'm not going back! Your mother has been stealing those golden apples from our garden. I was the one who wounded her last night, and now I'm here to finish what I started."

With these words, he burst into the house and cut the dragon's head off in one quick motion. Shortly afterwards, he rounded up the dragon's daughters and the four of them went back to where the rope was still hanging. The eldest daughter went up first, followed by the middle one. Now it was his turn to go up with the youngest girl.

"If you go first, my brothers will start a fight over you because you're the most beautiful of the three. If I go first, they won't feel like pulling you up later, and you probably wouldn't want to stay down here alone. So you go first. If my brothers love me, they'll pull me up, too."

"Take this ring," said the girl. "It's a gift from my heart, even though you killed our mother. If your brothers start fighting over me, I'll ask them to make magic clothes for me. Whoever can do that will become my husband. You wait here. If your brothers

refuse to pull you up, you'll stay here awhile and then fall through to the Lower Land. There, you will see two rams grazing there, one white, and the other one black. If you land on the white one, it will bring you all the way up to where we are. If you fall on the back of the black ram, though, it will take you all the way to the bottom of the Lower Land. I don't know how you'd be able to come back from there."

The young man tied the rope around the girl's waist, and his brothers pulled her out of the crevice. He waited a while for them to pull him up as well, but they didn't. All of a sudden, the ground under his feet gave way, and he plummeted down to the black ram which promptly took him to the bottom of the Lower Land. The young man decided to walk around and eventually got to a small house where he saw a frail old woman. She was kneading dough but instead of water, she was mixing the flour with hot, salty tears.

"Why are you using tears, grandma?" he asked, astonished.

"What else could I do?" she replied. "Our only well is barred by a giant dragon who doesn't let us get fresh water unless we sacrifice our daughters to him. I had six, and they all went there. There are no more maidens in the whole kingdom. The only one left is the king's daughter, and she's getting sacrificed today."

"Don't worry, grandma!" soothed the young man. "I'll save you from that monster. Just tell me how to get to the well." When he got there, he found the king's daughter crying.

"Don't be afraid! I'll defeat the dragon, and you'll be spared! There'll be no more sacrifices!" he promised. The two of them sat near the well and started chatting quietly. After a while, the young man dozed off with his head in the girl's lap. At sundown, the tall rock behind the well split in half, and a giant dragon roared out. The girl started crying again, and one of her tears fell on the young man's face and woke him up. He swiftly jumped up and lunged at the beast with his knife, but the beast was stronger and managed to drive him halfway into the ground. Luckily, he didn't give up but pulled himself out and cut the dragon's head off in one move. As soon as the monster died, the well filled up with clear, cool water.

When the young man took the king's daughter back to the palace, the king told him that half of the kingdom was now his as a reward for his bravery.

"I don't need the kingdom, Your Highness!" the young man said. "There's nothing I need here in the Lower Land. All I want is to go back to the Upper Land where I live."

The king was baffled at the request. “I don’t know how to help you do that. If you can get someone to take you all the way up there, I’ll provide everything else you need.”

The young man asked around and found an old man who advised him to go to the outskirts of the town.

“You’ll see a tall tree with a huge eagle’s nest on top. The mother-eagle has been trying to raise little ones for three years now, but a huge dragon always eats them up. Talk to her, maybe she can help you. “

The young man found the tree and sat underneath. Suddenly, the baby eagles’ sharp cry pierced the air. When he looked up, he saw a three-headed snake slithering towards the nest. He jumped up and sliced all three heads off in one movement. Just then, the mother-eagle came back to feed her young and heard their cries. Thinking that the man was harming them, she attacked him with her sharp beak.

“Don’t do that, Mother!” the baby eagles shouted. “This man saved us from the big snake!”

When the mother-eagle saw the severed snake heads on the ground, she asked the young man what she could do to repay him.

“Take me to the Upper Land!” he pleaded.

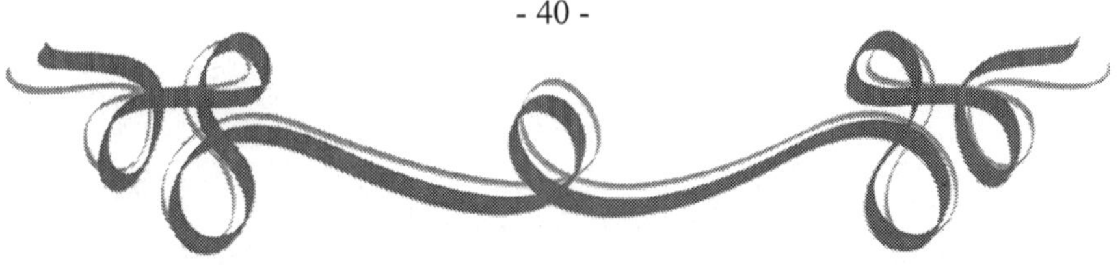

“That’s difficult,” replied the eagle, “but we can try. Find nine barren cows. Feed me their meat and give me fresh water from the well for nine weeks. Then, fill a barrel with pieces of meat and a barrel with fresh water, hang them off my back, sit on top, and we’ll see what happens.”

For nine weeks, the young man did everything as requested, and then the two of them started their long journey to the Upper Land. Along the way, he fed the mother-eagle and gave her plenty of water whenever she asked. This went on until there was no more meat left in the barrel. The next time the eagle asked for food, the young man cut a piece from his leg and gave it to her. The second time he gave the eagle a bit from his arm. Finally, the two of them reached the Upper Land, and the eagle landed, but the young man didn’t move from where he was sitting.

“Why aren’t you getting off my back and walking, my friend?” the eagle inquired.

“I can’t,” he replied, pointing at the spots from where he had cut the meat. “It hurts.”

The mother-eagle immediately opened her mouth, pulled the pieces from under her tongue, and gave them to the young man. He put them back in place and the wounds healed instantly, so he was

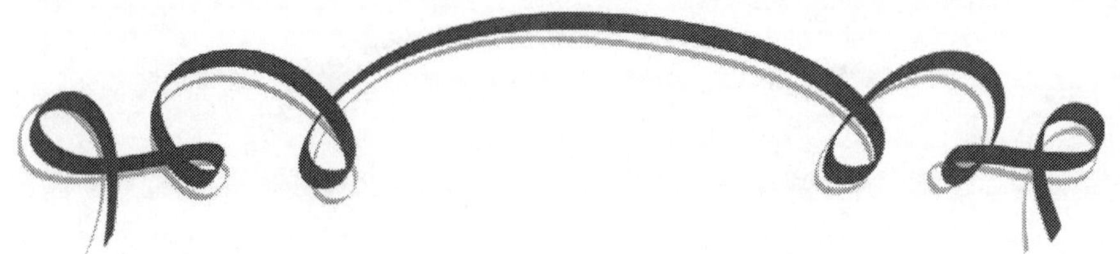

no longer hurting and was full of energy. The eagle then flew back to her babies, and the young man went home. When he got there, he saw that his brothers were still fighting over the girls. Each wanted the youngest one because she was also the most beautiful of the three.

"I'll marry whichever one of you can make magic clothes for me," she declared. The elder brothers were baffled but the youngest pulled out the special ring, and touched a walnut with it. The walnut cracked open revealing beautiful magic clothes inside. The youngest girl was satisfied. She married the youngest brother who was brave, smart, and kindhearted, and they lived happily ever after.

TALES ABOUT ANIMALS

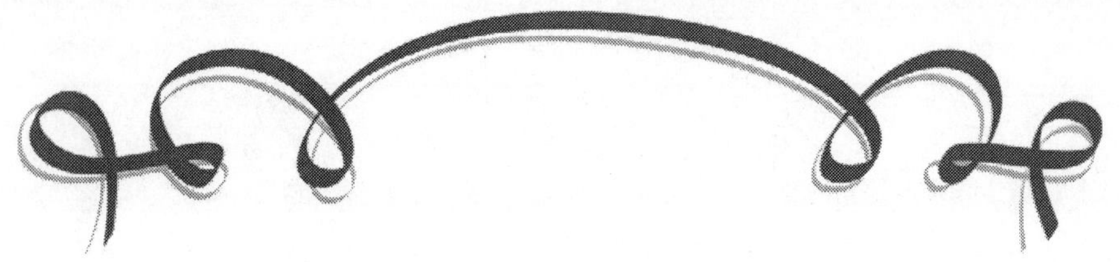

THE MAN AND THE SNAKE
(And why they are no longer friends)

Once upon a time, there was a man who had a beautiful vineyard. He was very proud of it and worked there every day. In the middle of the vineyard, under a huge pile of rocks, lived a big snake. The man discovered it and decided to do something good for it. One morning, he brought a bowl of fresh milk and left it by the rock pile. Sometime later, the snake came out, sniffed at the milk, and drank it. When the man went to check, he found a shiny golden coin in the empty dish. From that day on, he took a bowl of milk to the snake's hideaway every day and always found a shiny golden coin in return.

Many years went by. The vineyard owner got old and frail and couldn't tend to the property by himself. He called his son to help and explained to him about his long-standing arrangement with the snake. When the son got to the vineyard and saw the huge rock pile, he thought to himself, "There must be a lot of golden coins under there. Why don't I just kill the snake and take them all."

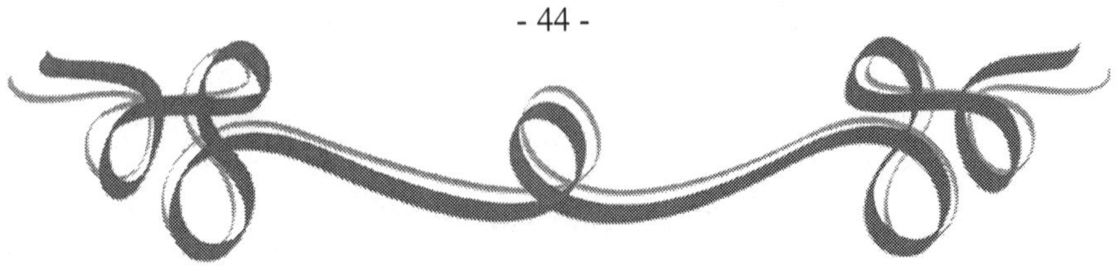

A few days later, he took a bowl of milk to the rocks and hid by the side, armed with a big, heavy stick. When the snake emerged and started drinking the milk, the young man hit it with the stick but managed only to tear off a part of its tail. The snake was enraged and immediately bit him. He returned home all swollen from the snakebite and told his father exactly what had happened. Soon after that, he succumbed to the poison and passed away.

After a period of mourning, the old man went to tend his vineyard again. He went to the huge rock pile and stood there, lost in memories of his late son. Suddenly, the snake slithered out and looked at him.

"Can we make peace and be friends like we used to?" the man asked.

"No way!" hissed the snake angrily. "For as long as you have your son's grave to look at, and I have my maimed tail hurting, there can never be friendship between us! When one does something, one must always think of the consequences."

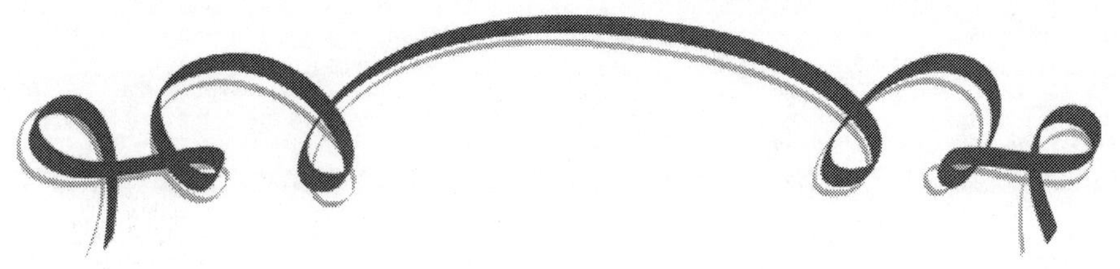

WHY THE VIXEN AND THE STORK ARE NO LONGER FRIENDS

Back when the stork and the vixen were still friends, they often visited each other's houses. One day, the stork invited the vixen over for lunch and served her a big jug full of milk.

"Welcome to my home, darling!" the stork crooned. "Let's have a little lunch together! As I'm a lonely bachelor, this won't be as good as anything a woman could make, but it's an offering from the heart. Let's enjoy!"

The jug was tall and narrow-mouthed, and the vixen couldn't reach the milk inside. She turned this way and that, tried to tip it over, licked the rim, but to no avail. Then she tried to stick her head inside, but it was too big for the narrow opening. The stork, on the other hand, had no problem getting his long beak inside the jug, and he drank all the milk, sip by sip. The vixen had to go home hungry.

A few days later, she invited the stork over for dinner. She made porridge and served it in a big, shallow pan. "Welcome to my home, dear friend!" she exclaimed. "Let's eat and catch up!"

The stork tried to slurp the porridge, but his long, sharp beak only succeeded in denting the pan. The vixen had no such problems. She reached down and slowly licked the pan clean. A little later, the stork got up to leave and said, “My dear, when you visited me, you ate well and had your fill. To tell you the truth, I’m leaving your home hungry today.”

“That’s where you’re wrong, my friend,” replied the vixen. ”When you were poking the pan with your beak, the whole neighborhood heard how you’re getting stuffed. When I was at your place, I left hungry.”

The stork got all flustered and left in silence. Since that day, there has been no love lost between him and the vixen.

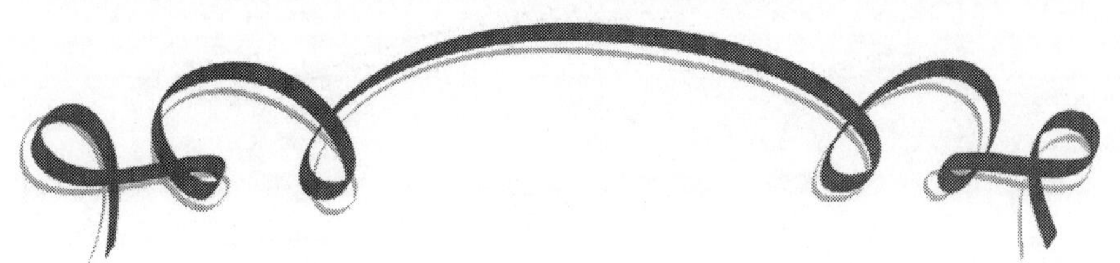

TALES WITH A MORAL

HOW THE ELDERLY CAME TO BE REVERED

Once upon a time, in a faraway kingdom, the cruel ruler ordered all the elderly people put to death. They were weak, couldn't work, and weren't much use, the king claimed. The king's father tried to change his mind, begged and pleaded, but to no avail. The king ordered that if anyone let their elderly parents live, they would face the most severe punishment. No one dared rebel, the elderly got killed, and a pall fell over the land. Only one young duke left his elderly father alive. He dug an underground hiding place and put him there. Every day, the duke would come down to talk to his father and ask his advice on various matters.

The king's father often told the king that all of his royal advisors are too young, inexperienced, and not fit to rule the kingdom. The young king got tired of listening to this and set out to show his father that young people had wits too. One day, he gathered his advisers and ordered, "Tomorrow at sunrise come here and show me how to weave a rope of sand." Everyone left with a heavy heart, as they had no one to ask for help. The young duke

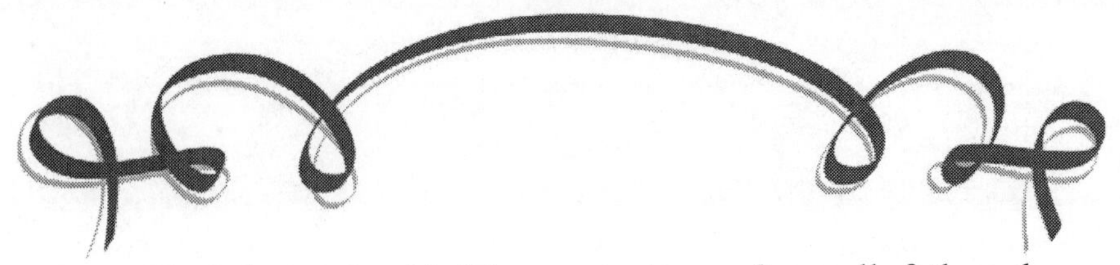

went to his father and said, “I’ve come to say farewell, father, the king’s going to have us all killed tomorrow.”

“Why would he do that?” wondered the elderly man. ”You’re all young, strong, and good at work and war.”

“He’ll kill us just the same,” answered the duke. “We’re to gather at sunrise and show him how to weave a rope of sand.”

“That’s very easy!” smiled the elderly father, and told him what to do.

The next day, nobody had anything to say except the young duke: “Your Highness, have a barrow of sand brought in, and I’ll weave the rope for you.”

When the sand arrived, the duke told the king, “Now, Your Highness, hold this end of the rope while I weave the rest.” The king acknowledged the duke’s wit and let everyone go free.

A few days went by and the king decided to test his advisors again. “You’re to come here tomorrow at sunrise,” he said, “and tell me where the sun shines first.”

The royal advisors were stumped for an answer; the duke ran to his father and told him about the king’s riddle. The next morning, everyone gathered in the palace. When the king asked if anybody knew the answer, deep silence fell over the room.

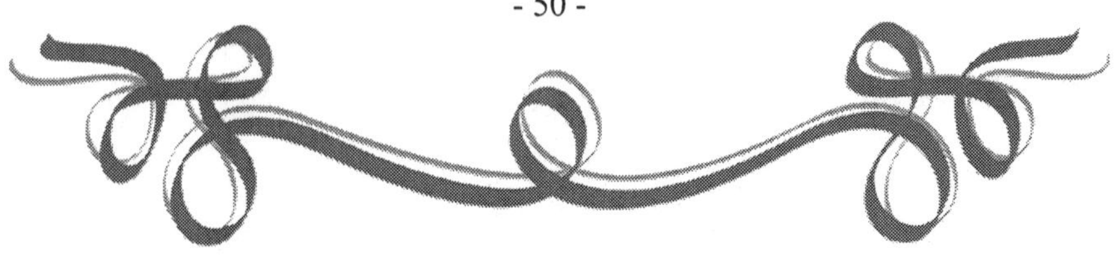

“How could you not know?” raged the king.

“Well, the sun rises from the east,” said someone.

“Not true, Your Highness!” exclaimed the young duke, “The sun first shines to the west. Look at the mountain tops to the west of us, that’s where you’ll see it first.”

Everyone turned to the west and saw that even before the sun rose from the east, all the mountaintops to the west were already bathed in its golden glow. The king realized that the duke was the smartest person in the land and proudly proclaimed that all young people were smart.

Years went by. Anarchy swept the nation. The young people stopped cultivating the land and raising cattle. Drought destroyed the crops, hail demolished the vegetables, and bad times arrived everywhere. People were starving. The few, who had some grain stashed away, had long since eaten the last of it. The king got scared. What was he to do? He gathered his advisors and ordered them to leave no stone unturned but find some grain for seed. They went away and looked high and low but found no grain. A week went by. The young duke, who had hidden his elderly father, went to him and asked for forgiveness, as he was sure the king would have them killed come morning.

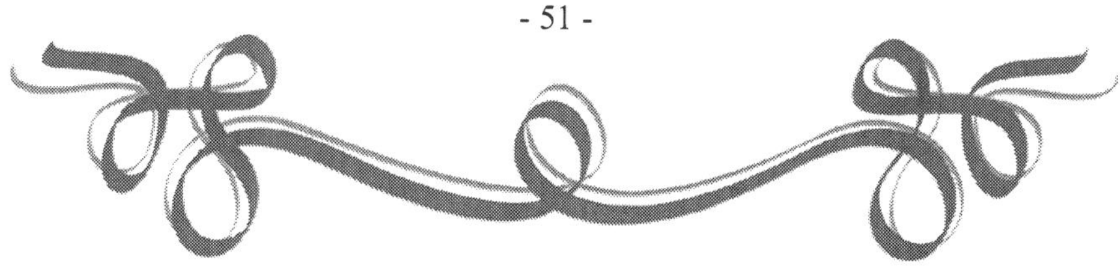

"Don't be afraid, son," said the father, "this is the easiest thing. Tell the king to dig the anthills, he'll find plenty of grain there."

When he got to the palace, the young duke found the others looking sad, expecting to be punished.

"Your Highness," he said, "I beg you, don't kill your advisors. I know where we can find grain."

"Where? How do you know? Who told you?"

"Inside the anthills, Your Highness. There's a lot of grain there."

"How did you know that?" marveled the king. "You're the only one who solved my other riddles, too. Tell me, did you think of this yourself, or did someone advise you?"

"I'm afraid to tell you, Your Highness! If I tell you, you'll order me killed."

The king swore he wouldn't do that, as he was curious to find out the truth.

"When my father grew old, I didn't want to kill him, so I hid him and have been taking care of him ever since. He taught me what to say about the sand rope and about the sunrise, and now

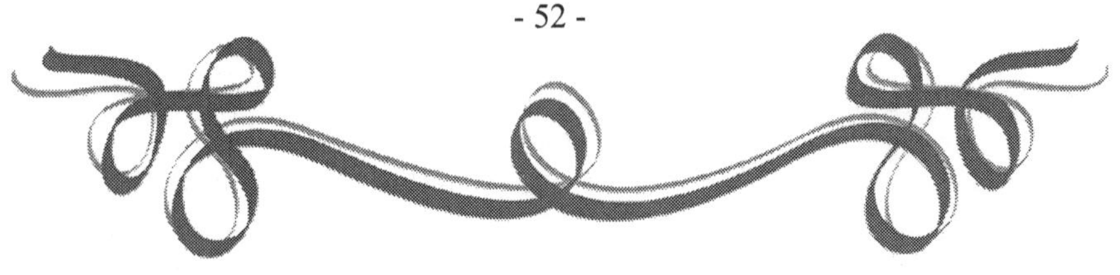

about the grain. Every time I went to him with a problem, he would smile and say, 'That's the easiest thing!'"

The king listened carefully, then issued a new order: the elderly people were not to be killed anymore but to be cared for and protected.

Later, the anthills were dug, lots of grain was found, and the kingdom was saved from famine. And that's how it came to be that the elderly were to always be revered.

A GIFT FROM THE HEART

A long time ago in a land far away, three brothers decided to leave their home and go in search of better jobs and more money. They packed and started their journey down the wide country road. Toward the end of the day, the brothers got to a crossroad.

"We'll split here, and each of us will take a different road," instructed the eldest brother. "You take the right side," he said to the middle brother, "and you, our youngest brother, will take the middle one. We'll meet again here in three years' time, on the first day of spring, and compare our gains."

The brothers bid each other good-bye and left. The eldest brother reached a big city where he found work in a bakery, and in three years managed to amass sizeable wealth. The middle brother opened a roadhouse tavern next to a well-traveled bridge. He also made a very good living and saved a great deal of money. The youngest brother hired himself out as a helping hand to an elderly shepherd. When the three years were out, he went to collect his wages. The old shepherd provided a purse full of money, and put three walnuts next to it.

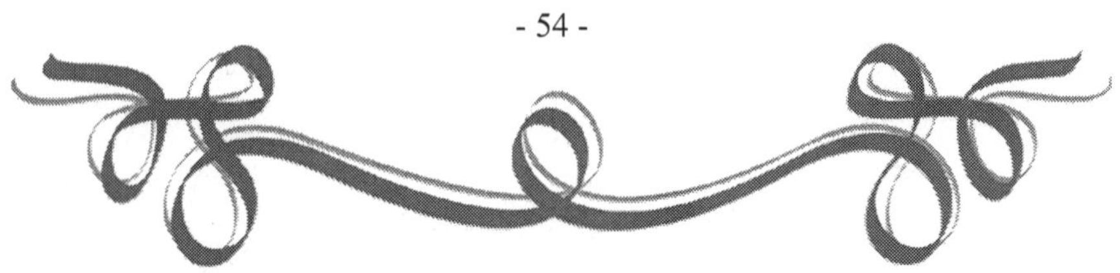

“I’m a tired, ailing old man,” he said. “I can’t chase the sheep like I used to. If it weren’t for you, my herd would have perished. I’m very grateful for your good work. For your services, I can pay you either the money, or these three walnuts. The money doesn’t come from my heart because it’s like fire; it’s easy to get burned on it. But the walnuts are a gift from my heart. It’s your choice.”

The young man gave the offer some thought and decided to go for the walnuts. He pocketed them and left with the old shepherd’s blessing.

On the first day of spring, the three brothers met again at the designated crossroad.

“How did you fare?” asked the eldest.

“Very well,” replied the middle brother. The two of them opened their purses and started counting. The youngest produced the three walnuts out of his pocket. “This is what I earned.” he said. “It’s a gift from the heart.”

The elder brothers were enraged, “Hey, we’ve seen some stupid people, but you beat them all! You must be the dumbest person on earth! How could you accept three measly walnuts as pay for three years of hard work?! Go back to that shepherd and claim

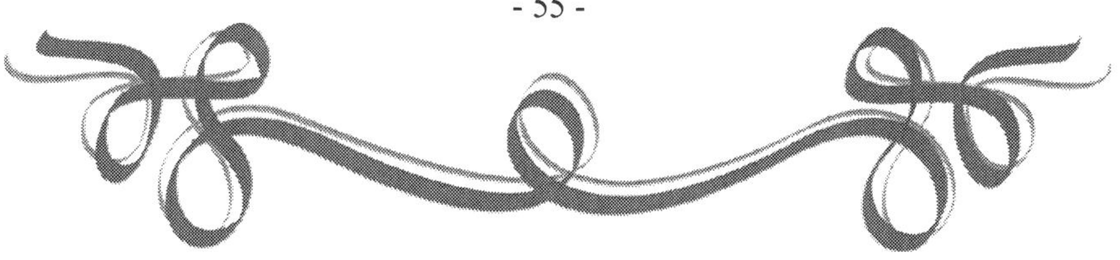

your rightful wages, or else don't bother to come back to live with us!"

Saddened, the youngest brother turned to go back. "Here I was, thinking that a gift from the heart was the best, and look what happened." After a while, he got hungry and decided to break one of the walnuts and eat it. When the shell cracked open, it suddenly grew as big as a giant oak barrel, and a great big herd of sheep, little lambs, and handsome rams emerged from the inside. The young man was overjoyed and decided to check the second walnut as well. When he broke it open, a pair of young bulls came out, pulling a brand new cart with a shiny steel plow attached to it. "This is incredible!" he exclaimed, and turned to lead the herd and the bulls back to his home.

Just before entering the village, the young man cracked open the last walnut. Bright light spilled from inside, and a beautiful young woman came out.

"Take me to your home!" she said. "I'm a fairy maiden, and I'm destined to be your wife."

The young man helped her get on the cart and they continued on, accompanied by the jingling of bells from the huge herd. When his elder brothers saw the livestock, the new cart, and the gorgeous

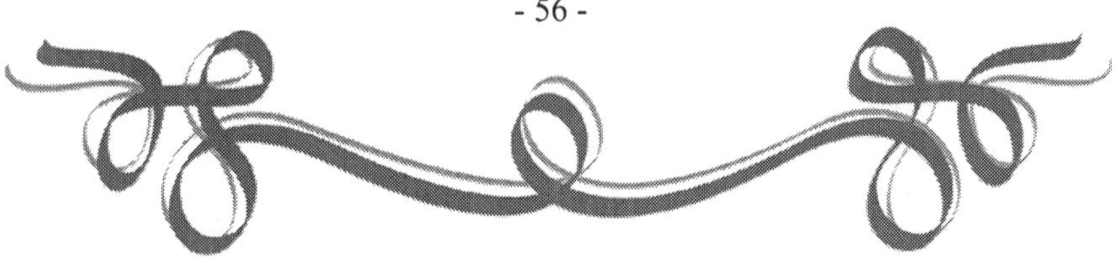

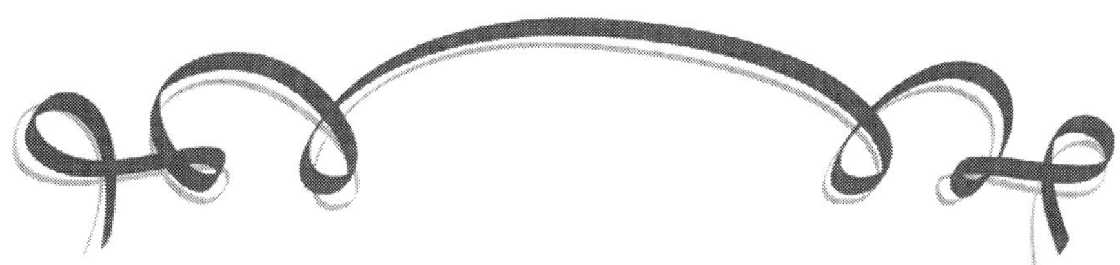

maiden, they were struck speechless. It had finally dawned on them that there was nothing more precious than a gift from the heart.

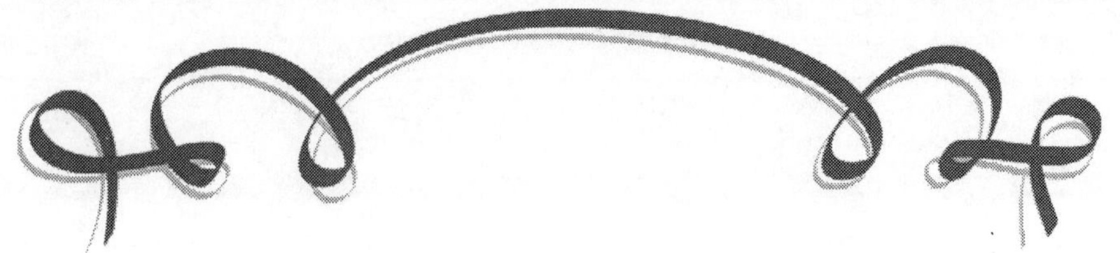

PRECIOUS WORDS

Once upon a time, there lived a poor man. He had been working as a servant in a wealthy household for twenty years. On his last day, the master called him in and showed him a purse full of money. “These are your wages. You can take it all. And this,” the man said, holding out three golden coins, “is a gift from the heart. Take one or the other.”

After giving the matter some thought, the man took the three golden coins, bid the master farewell, and left. Along the way, he encountered three men, two of whom were chatting away, and the third one was silent.

“Why isn’t your friend talking?” he inquired.

“Because he wants one golden coin each time he speaks,” they replied.

“Well, I’m poor anyway. Here’s a coin, let’s see what he has to say.”

The silent guy took the coin and said, “Don’t wade in murky water.”

A while later, the poor man gave the silent stranger his second coin.

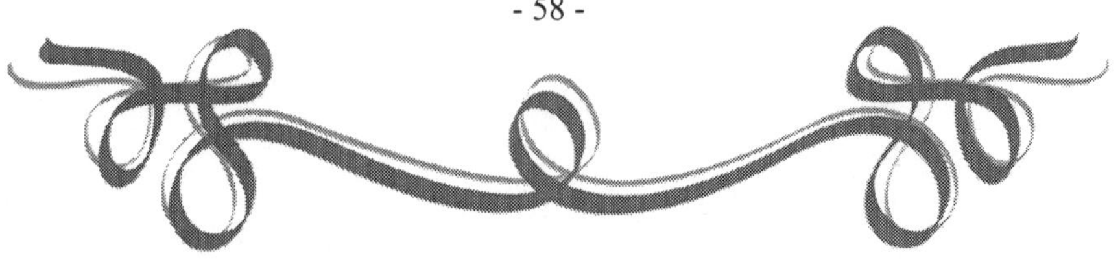

"When you see eagles circling over something, go check it out," he advised. The poor man was surprised by this advice but curiosity got the best of him and he offered his last coin for one more advice.

"Whatever you do, think twice before you do it," said the silent guy.

Some time later, the foursome got to a crossroad and separated. The poor man walked for a long time and eventually got to a big river. The water ran deep and was murky, and he was afraid to go across. A traveling merchant on a horse came by and asked, "Why aren't you crossing the river, my friend?"

"I don't wade in murky waters," he replied.

The merchant laughed and spurred his horse into the water. When they reached the middle of the river, the animal got frightened, threw his rider off, and he drowned. When the horse got out, there were two big bags full of gold tied to the saddle. The poor man hopped on the horse and continued his journey. Suddenly, he spotted a couple of eagles circling above a tall rock in the distance. Remembering the stranger's second advice, he went to investigate and found five dangerous-looking men, all dead. It occurred to him

that they must have killed each other over the parceling of fresh loot, so he looked around and found loads of precious goods.

After several more hours of riding, the man reached his home. Through the uncurtained window, he saw his wife talking to a stranger. His first impulse was to shoot the man but he recalled the silent stranger's advice and gave the situation some thought. Just at that moment, the unfamiliar-looking man looked at his wife and said, "Mother, it has been twenty years since my father went away. I'm going to look for him tomorrow." Upon hearing this, the man happily knocked on the door and was met by his wife and grown son who both rejoiced at his arrival.

One day, the son said to his father, "Father, I want to become a traveling merchant." The father gave him 1000 golden coins and instructed him, "Wherever you go, don't engage in conversation with young people." The young man kissed respectfully his father's hand and bid him good-bye. On the third day of his journey, he passed by a cemetery where three men were pounding on a freshly dug grave, and asked them why they were doing so.

"We're merchants, and he owed us 1000 golden coins. Now he's dead. How are we ever going to get our money back?"

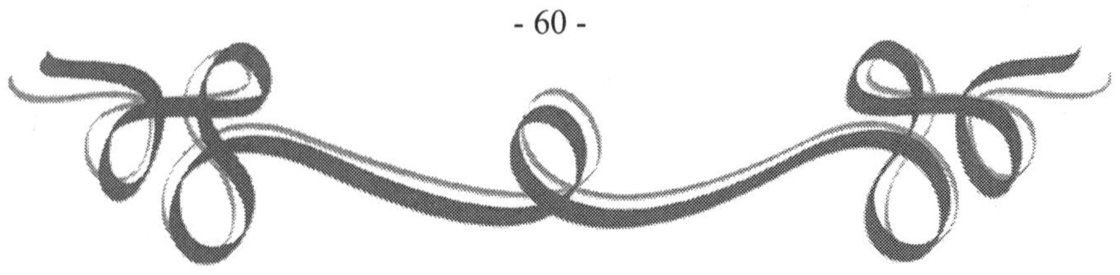

The young man gave the men his 1000 golden coins and returned home.

"You did the right thing," said his father. "Take these 3000 golden coins now, and go again. And remember, don't engage in conversation with young people."

The son traveled a whole day without stopping and by nightfall arrived at an inn. He saw an elderly man sitting in the corner of the front room and went over to greet him. The old man learned that the boy was lonesome and agreed to accompany him in his travels. In the morning, the pair of them set out on their way and soon arrived to a big kingdom. With each new day the princess of that kingdom got married but the grooms were always found dead the following morning. Finally, the king announced that whoever managed to survive the wedding night with his daughter would become her husband.

"Do you want to become the king's son-in-law?" asked the old man.

"I do but I'm afraid I'll die like the others before me," said the boy.

"As long as I'm with you, have no fear," said the old man.

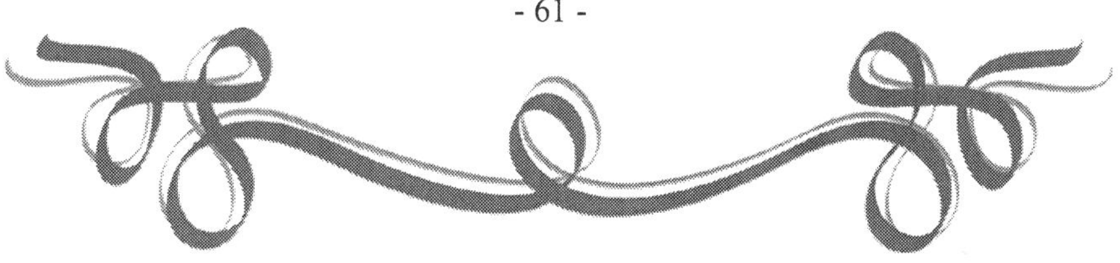

Together, they went to see the king. "Greetings, Your Highness! We heard that no groom had survived the wedding night with your daughter. My boy here wishes to become your son-in-law."

"Let him try," agreed the king. "If he lives through the night, I'll give him half of the kingdom as well."

"Go buy a sack and a pair of scissors," asked the old man. The wedding was lavish and joyous. In the evening, the old man pulled the boy aside, "Don't go to bed until I come in. When I tell you, 'Sweet dreams!', then you can sleep."

The old man bid the young couple good night but didn't leave; instead, he became invisible and stood next to the headboard of the bed. When the newlyweds started dozing off, a giant three-headed snake slithered down from the ceiling. It was about to bite the boy's forehead when the old man cut its heads off and stashed them in the sack he was holding. He then woke up the young couple and wished them sweet dreams.

The king was very happy that his new son-in-law had survived. He threw an immense feast and gave to the young man half of the kingdom as a present.

"I don't want your kingdom!" the young man said. "I wanted a beautiful wife and I got her."

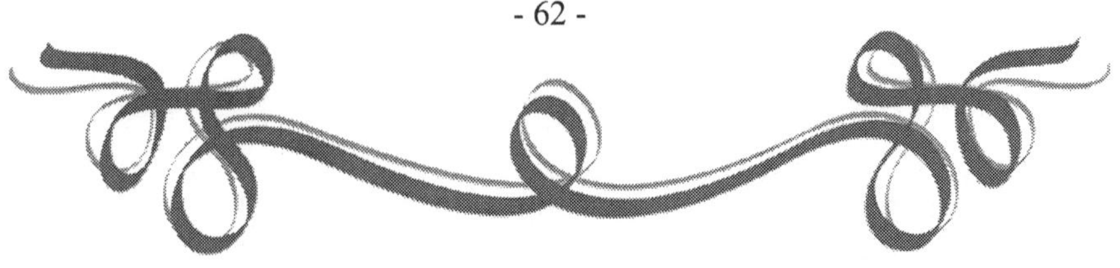

The young couple and the old man lived happily in the palace for a while. Then the young man got homesick. They bid the king good-bye and, laden with all kinds of precious gifts, set off toward the boy's village. After a whole week of traveling, the three of them reached that same cemetery. The old man got off his horse and said, "Well, my son, we've gathered enough riches. We gained them together and must now divide them evenly."

"Of course, we'll divide them evenly as you say," the young man agreed. The old man smiled at him then and said, "I'm the one for whose relief you paid when those men were pounding on my grave. I was in a lot of pain and am very grateful to you for your good deed. Take all this bounty for yourself and go in peace." As he said that, the old man gave the newlyweds his blessing and climbed down into the waiting grave. The young couple went back to the village, reunited with the boy's parents, and they all lived happily ever after.

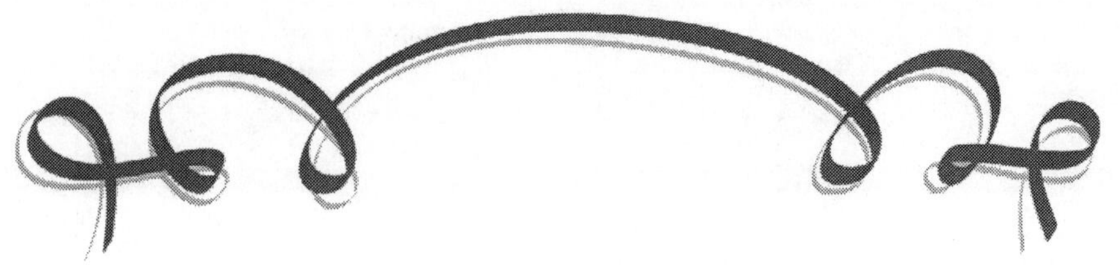

THE MOST PRECIOUS THING

Once upon a time, there lived a king who had three beautiful daughters whom he loved very much. As any father, the king, too, wanted to give his children good upbringing, teach them good values, and marry them into prominent, wealthy families.

One day, the king was sitting around, playing with the girls. When they got tired of playing and sat next to him, he asked his eldest daughter, “Tell me, darling, how much do you love me?”

“I love you as much as gold, Father,” the girl replied.

“Since you love me that much, we’ll marry you to the wealthiest duke in the land, and you’ll always be surrounded by riches”, said the king, and turned to his middle daughter. “What about you? How much do you love me?”

“I love you as much as honey and precious stones, Father,” she replied.

“Since you love me that much, my dear, we’ll marry you into a wealthy kingdom where you’ll always have plenty to eat and wear,” promised the king. “And how about you, little one?”

“I love you as much as salt, Father!” exclaimed the little girl.

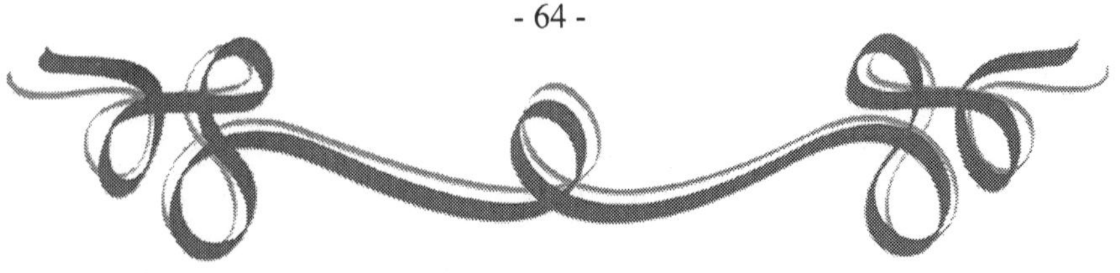

"As much as salt, you say? So you don't love me at all!" shouted the angry king. "It's a pity we wasted time raising you! From now on, you're not my daughter! Go away and never come back! I don't need you anymore!"

When the queen heard this, she got frightened and wanted to smooth things out, but the king was adamant and the youngest daughter was banished.

Years went by. The elder daughters got married into wealthy families, the youngest was long forgotten. Meanwhile, she was alive and well. When her father, the king, drove her away, the girl walked about the town for a while and met a poor kind old man, leading a donkey. She offered to help him, and he asked who she was and where she lived. When the girl said that she had no parents and was all alone in the world, the old man offered to take her in.

His home was right next to the neighboring kingdom, and the young prince often went there to hunt. He was polite and modest and often sat down to rest and have a word with the old man. One day, he saw the girl, fell instantly in love, and wanted to marry her. His father, the king, was reluctant as the girl was the daughter of a poor old man, but the prince threatened to become a monk if he

couldn't marry her, so the king went to see her and decide for himself.

When he got to the old man's house, a neatly dressed young girl came out to greet him. The king figured out that this was the girl his son liked, and asked if her father was home.

"My grandfather isn't here," she answered. "I'm by myself."

"Where's your father then?"

"I don't have a father anymore," she replied. "He sent me away from our palace a long time ago."

The king was intrigued, "Which palace?" And she told him the whole story.

The king was a smart man and instantly realized that the girl loved her father the most, but he, being greedy, didn't appreciate her. He went back to his palace and sent his son to ask for her hand in marriage.

The wedding was big and festive. A lot of guests from many kingdoms came; the girl's father was invited as well. The spread was lavish, the tables were groaning heavily under all the delicious foods. To teach the bride's father a lesson, the king ordered that he be served dishes that were cooked with no salt at all. The girl's father tried one course after another, but couldn't eat any of them:

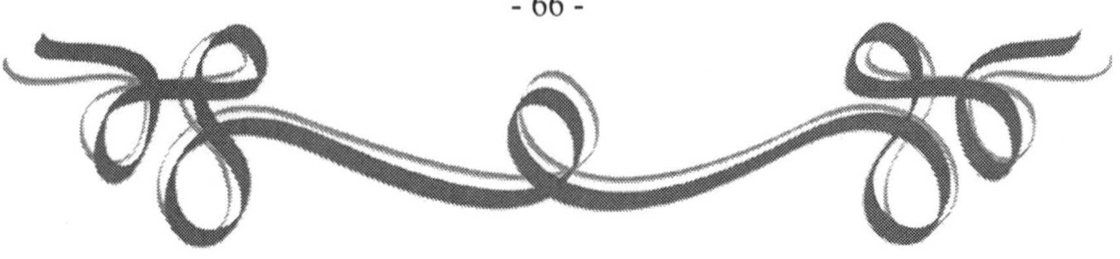

even though the tableware was encrusted with gemstones and all the dishes looked very appetizing, they were all smothered with honey.

The girl's father was hungry and complained to his new in-law, "Why are you trying to starve me?"

"Starve you?! The table's covered with delicious food, everything's served on exquisite platters with gemstones on them, and you've been given knives and forks made of sterling silver. If you're hungry, eat, that's what the food's for."

"You're making fun of me, aren't you!" raged the father. "Nobody eats gold, silver, and gemstones, and roasted meat shouldn't swim in honey! Give me some salt, that's the only way to fix this food."

"Aha, so you can't eat without salt, can you?" asked the groom's father. "Why, then, did you send your daughter away like an orphan? You spoiled your elder daughters because they loved you like gold, silver, and honey, all those things that people could live without."

"How do you know this?" asked the girl's father, very surprised.

"I know it from my daughter-in-law, the bride; she's your youngest daughter. She loved you the most, but you were blinded by greed and didn't see it."

The girl's father realized then that salt was the most precious thing in the world. Many people live happily without riches and without ever having tasted honey, but without salt, there's no life. It became clear to him that his elder daughters didn't truly love him, so he disowned them and bequeathed the kingdom to the youngest daughter.

BIG CHILL, LITTLE CHILL, AND GRANNY MARCH

January and February have long been the two coldest months of the year. Once upon a time, people thought of them as brothers: January, being longer, got to be known as Big Chill, and February, being shorter, was nicknamed Little Chill. The month of March, in contrast, brings gentle sun and delicate flowers, and that's why people started thinking of it as a woman and nicknamed it Granny March.

Granny March was the little sister of Big Chill and Little Chill. The three owned a big vineyard together. Every fall, they picked the fragrant grapes and made three barrelfuls of wine, one for each of them.

Big Chill spent every day outdoors. He went up and down hills, climbed mountains and explored big open fields. He came home in the evenings tired and windblown, covered in snow and ice, and thoroughly frozen. To warm up, he always had some wine with his dinner, and so, little by little, his barrel got emptied.

Little Chill, just like his elder brother, spent his days roaming around the countryside. He cracked the thick ice over

rivers so fish could swim freely, cleaned debris from forests, pointed floods away from people's dwellings, and built nests for little birds. At the end of the day, he came home exhausted and liked to have some wine with his meal. Little by little, his barrel got emptied, too.

When the brothers were invited to somebody's wedding, they felt bad about not having any wine to take along. Meanwhile, their sister's barrel sat untouched and full in her cellar. Big Chill and Little Chill thought about it and decided that she wouldn't notice if they started drinking some of her wine. Whenever they needed some, one or the other would come to Granny March's house and stealthily pour out a glass or two. This went on for quite a while, until one day her barrel was emptied out.

A few days later, Granny March got busy preparing for spring. She tidied things up, planted flowers, and by the end of the day, was very tired. She made herself dinner and went down to the cellar to get a glass of wine. To her immense surprise, there wasn't even a drop of wine in the big barrel. It was bone dry and had started falling apart at the seams.

It dawned on Granny March then that her brothers had taken advantage of her wine. She was so mad at them that she threw things, yelled, and cried rivers before finally calming herself down

and beginning to smile a little. “So what if they drank all my wine!” she thought. “They’re my brothers, not strangers, after all.”

Granny March stopped being sad and was no longer angry with her brothers, but, deep down, she still felt hurt by their dishonesty. Some days, she thought about it and her tears flowed freely. At other days, her mood was joyful and her eyes sparkled with happiness. And that’s why the weather in March is so changeable and makes us wear short sleeves but have umbrellas handy.

TALES ABOUT WIT AND WISDOM

THE WITTY MAIDEN

Once upon a time in a far-away land, there lived a man who wanted to find a perfect match for his son. None of the eligible girls in the village appealed to him because they weren't smart enough. In the fall, when the wedding season began, the father decided to go around the neighboring villages and search for a match there. He traveled far and was already thinking of turning back empty handed when an old woman told him of a beautiful witty maiden who lived a few villages away. The man thanked her and a short time later was knocking on the young maiden's door.

She had a large family — parents and grandparents, but only her mother was at home, mending shirts by the fireplace.

"Welcome to our home!" she enthused. "Come in and take a load off!"

"Are you alone?" he inquired.

"Yes, everyone's out at the wheatfield, working. Only my mom is here. What brings you to our village?"

"Nothing special, I was just passing through and decided to stop by for a rest and a glass of water."

The young woman brought the guest a glass of cold water, and he drank it while thinking of ways to test whether she was as smart and witty as everyone claimed.

"Do you have a father?" he asked.

"Yes, I do."

"Where is he?"

"He's at the mill, grinding wheat for flour."

"Is he going to come home soon, or will he be long?"

"Well," she replied, "If he takes the short way, he'll be long. But if he takes the long way, he'll be home shortly."

The man couldn't make heads or tails of her answer and stared at her in amazement. Meanwhile, the young women had figured out that he was testing her and was eagerly awaiting the next question.

"Do you have a grandfather?"

"Yes, I do."

"Where is he?"

"Out on the wheatfield."

"What's he doing there?"

"Spilling one and making two."

The man couldn't figure that answer out either.

“So, you have a grandma?”

“Yes, I do.”

“Where is she?”

“At the neighbor’s house.”

“What is she doing there?”

“She’s doing to him something that she has never done to him before and will never again.”

The man racked his brain but couldn’t understand that reply either.

“Do you have a mother?”

“Yes, I do.”

“Where is she?”

“She’s here, in the house.”

“What is she up to?

“Making one new from two old ones.”

The man had always considered himself smart, but the young woman’s responses left him baffled. “This young lady’s either very smart, or very crazy,” he thought. When he got back to his village, the man called a friend over and told him about the girl’s riddles. The friend was very impressed. “She’s the wittiest girl you’ll ever find!”

"But what do her answers mean?"

"Listen carefully," the friend explained. "She told you that her father would be home shortly if he took the long way, but that he would be long if he took the short way. It means that the shortcut goes up and down steep paths overgrown with prickly bushes and crosses through passes high up in the mountain. The roundabout roads are wider and smoother, easier to travel, and so her father would be home sooner."

The man was amazed. "So what did she mean about her grandfather?"

"Well, she told you that he was spilling one and making two, right? That's exactly true—her grandfather was sprinkling around and planting the grains from a sack of wheat. From that one sack of grain, he would get two at harvest time."

"What about the grandma?"

"Very easy. The girl told you that her grandmother was doing something to the neighbor that she had never done to him before and would never again. That means the neighbor had passed away, and she was there to close his eyes. She had never done that to him before and would never do it again."

"Now I understand!" exclaimed the man happily. "But what about her mother's making one new from two old ones?"

"She meant that her mom was mending shirts. She took the good parts from two old shirts and sewed them into a new one. Now, do you see how bright and witty this girl is?"

"Yes, I do!" smiled the man. "God bless you for helping me figure it out, my friend! Soon, you'll be an honored guest at my son's wedding to this girl!"

He went home and told his son about the very beautiful and very witty young maiden he had found for him to marry.

A week later, they were all dancing at the wedding. It went on for three days and three nights of good food, good wine, and lots of fun and riddles.

THE MAN WHO OUTWITTED THE KING

Once upon a time, there lived a king who had been ruling his kingdom for many years. One day, he decided to get a group of his closest advisors and mix with the ordinary people, see how they live. Together, they visited many villages and towns. Along the way, they encountered a wizened old man plowing his wheatfield.

"Good afternoon, my friend!" the king greeted him warmly.

"God bless, Your Highness!" replied the old man heartily.

"Has this mountain been covered in snow for a long time?"

"Thirty years now."

"Could you shear this herd of rams?"

"Sure I could! As soon as I can lay my hands on them!"

The king and his entourage bid the old man good-bye and continued on their way. Sometime later, the king inquired if anyone had figured out the old man's words.

"No, Your Highness, we haven't. You asked about snow on the mountain, but there was no mountain. Then you asked about a herd of rams, but there was no herd either.

"Think harder!" instructed the king. "If you can't figure it out soon, I'll fire you and hire that old man in your place."

The royal advisors thought long and hard for three days and nights but couldn't come up with anything, so they went back to ask the old man. "Tell us, old man, what did the king ask you?"
"Give me fifty golden coins each and I'll tell you," he responded.
The royal advisors had no choice but to pay him, and when they did, the old man spoke again, "The king asked whether my hair had turned white a long time ago and I told him 30 years now. Then he asked if I could shear a herd of rams, and I said yes. You are the rams, and I just sheared fifty golden coins off each of you."
Ashamed of themselves, the advisors departed silently.

The next day, the king and his sons went for a long walk in the countryside and met the same old man.

"God bless, old man!" greeted the king.

"God bless, Your Highness!"

"How are the distant ones?"

"Not distant at all these days."

"How are the thirty-two doing?

"Only six remain now."

"How are the two?"

“The two have become four.”

“If I send you two, can you fleece them?”

“Of course I can!”

On the way back to the palace, the king asked his sons, “What did the old man and I talk about?” They thought long and hard but couldn’t come up with an answer.

“You won’t be fit to inherit the kingdom and rule it until you can figure out what we talked about!” pronounced the king. “That old man would do a better job because he’s witty and smart.”

The king’s sons racked their brains over the puzzling exchange to no avail, and one morning, they went back to the old man.

“May you live a long and happy life, old man!” they said. “Please tell us, what exactly did you talk about with our father?”

“I’ll tell you gladly, but you’ll have to pay me one thousand golden coins each.”

The sons willingly counted out the money, and the old man explained, “The king asked how my eyes are doing, and I told him that I can’t see well anymore. Then he inquired about my teeth, and I told him that I now have only six left. When he asked how my legs are holding up, I explained that I’d started walking on all fours

—my two legs and two crutches. And when he asked if I could fleece the two, and I said yes, that meant you. I've taken one thousand golden coins from each of you, and that's fleecing, pure and simple."

The king's sons bowed their heads in shame and returned to the palace. A few days later, the king decided to visit the old man again and test his own wit.

"Don't you have sons to help you work the land, old man?" asked the king.

"I have three, Your Highness, but they aren't good at plowing."

"What do they do?"

"My eldest son takes money away from people but isn't a thief. The elder one begs but isn't a beggar. My youngest son cuts flesh but isn't a butcher."

"Why are you working the land on a holiday?"

"Because I make only three golden coins a day. I feed myself on one, pay a debt with the other, and reap interest with the third."

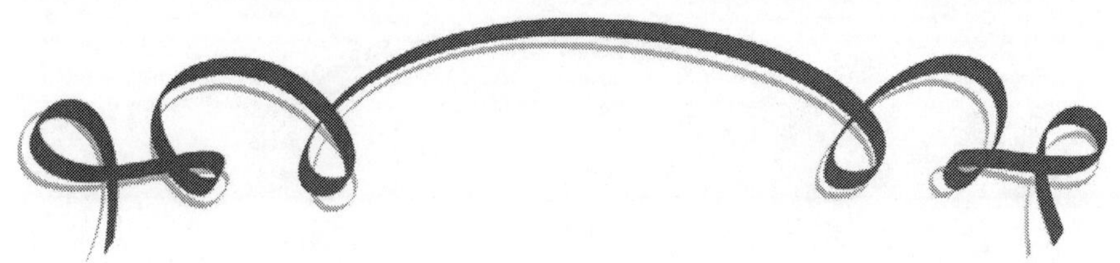

The king returned home and thought long and hard about the old man's riddles but couldn't crack them, so he went to the old man again and asked him to decipher his words.

"With pleasure, Your Highness! But you'll first have to pay me a sack of golden coins."

After the king paid up, the old man explained, "My eldest son is a lawyer, so he takes money from people but isn't a thief. My middle boy is a priest so he begs money for the church but isn't a beggar. And my youngest son is a surgeon so he cuts flesh but isn't a butcher. From the three golden coins I make every day, I feed myself on one, feed my mother with the second one—that's how I repay my duty as a son; and the third one goes to raising my children so it reaps interest. Now do you understand me, Your Highness?"

The king nodded, bid a respectful farewell to the smart old man, and, humbled, returned to his palace to continue ruling the kingdom.

THE POOR MAN AND THE DEVILS

Once upon a time in a small village, there lived a very poor man. When he died, he left nothing behind, and his son inherited only a ball of twine. Having no other choice, the young man took the ball and went in search of a better life. As he was walking along the road one day, one of his shoelaces fell apart. He pulled out the ball of twine and started making a new one. Lost in thought, the man suddenly realized he had reached the bank of a big river. He was looking around for a place to cross when there was a splash and a little devil came out of the water. "What are you doing?" the creature asked.

"Making a twine," the man replied.

"What for?"

"So I can tie the river up."

"Why do you want to tie the river up?"

"So I can carry it home with me!"

The little devil dived underwater and went to find its father, the big devil. "Father, there's a man up there on the river bank, who wants to tie our river up and carry it away!"

"One of our enemies must have concocted this," said the big devil. "Where would we live? I can't run with my one leg, but you can. Challenge him to a fight. You'll win, and he won't take our river away."

The little devil jumped out of the water and called out to the man, "What do you want?"

"If you can wrestle with me and win, you can take the river with you!"

"No problem," the man agreed, "but you'll have to come to my village with me."

"Sure I'll come!" exclaimed the little devil. "I'm not afraid of you!"

The two of them walked for a while and got to the dwelling of a huge dragon.

"My son lives here.You're a kid, and my son's a kid, so you'll wrestle with him while I watch," instructed the man.

When the dragon came out, the little devil screamed in terror and fled. When it got back into the river, the little devil found its father and complained bitterly, "I'm afraid to wrestle with this man! He has a son my age, but when he showed up, the forest shook."

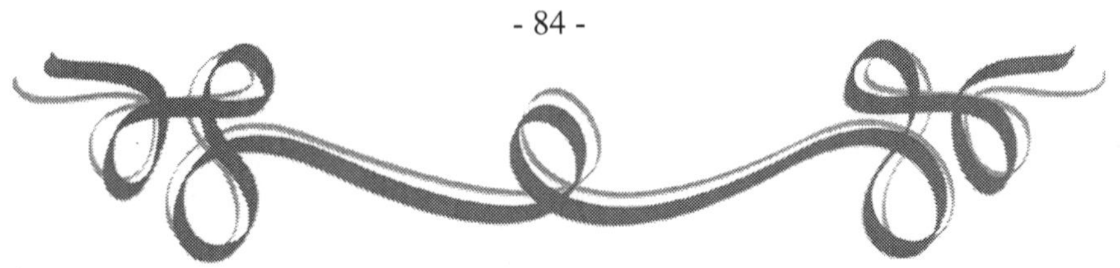

The big devil thought for a while and said, “Go to the man and challenge him to an apple-throwing contest! You’ll outthrow him, and our river will be safe.”

The little devil got inside an air bubble and swam to the surface. It found the man waiting and folding a piece of twine in two.

“Why are you folding the twine in two?” asked the little devil.

“To make it stronger,” answered the man.

“Why do you need to make it stronger?”

“So I can carry the river with it.”

“You can take the river away only if you outthrow me,” challenged the little devil.

“Deal,” agreed the man. ”You go first!”

The little devil threw the apple with all its might and the apple flew clear across the river. The man made as if to throw his apple but hid it in his bag instead. “You see that?” he laughed. “Your apple was in plain view while it was flying, and I saw where it landed. Mine, on the other hand, flew so high and landed so far away that nobody could see it.”

The little devil got frustrated and went back underwater. "He won, Father! Now he'll take our river away!"

"Are you joking?" the big devil was very puzzled.

"No, I'm not! He's getting ready to tie the river up now."

"Looks like I need to go deal with him," decided the big devil. "No way we are letting him take our home away!" He grabbed his crutches and hobbled up to the bank where the man was tying up his shoelaces.

"Hey you!" shouted the devil. "Why are you tying our river up?"

"So I can carry it with me," replied the man.

"It's our home! Where are we supposed to live?"

"I don't care if it's yours or not!" shouted the man. "You go live wherever you wish! If you and your son stay in the river, you'll be my slaves."

"Leave the river alone!" the big devil begged. "We'll give you a sack full of golden coins."

The man wasn't impressed. "One piddling sack? No way! It's not even worth carrying!"

"Alright then, how about two?" offered the devil. "And I'll carry them for you. "

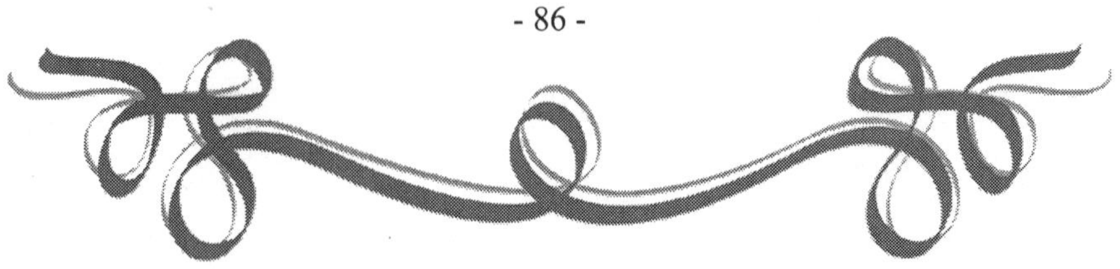

"That's better," agreed the man. "Make those sacks really big, and we have a deal."

The devil dived in the water and soon came out with two huge bags full of golden coins. The two of them set off toward the village, the man walking in front, and the devil trudging behind, laden with the heavy load.

"If the devil finds out where I live," mused the man, "he'll tell his friends, and they'll come to take my gold tomorrow." After thinking some more, the man started measuring the devil from head to toe.

"Why are you measuring me?" asked the devil, very surprised.

"My house is covered in devil hides," the man explained, "but there's a bare spot up on the roof, so I'm looking to see if your hide will be big enough to fit." As he said that, the man resumed measuring. The devil didn't want to wait any longer. He threw the bags of golden coins on the ground and ran back toward the river. The man picked up his riches and went back home. From that day on, he lived a very happy life and never lacked anything.

Made in the USA
Lexington, KY
21 August 2012